Father *Figure's*
❦ PROMISE ❧

Father Murphy's PROMISE

novelization by
LARRY WEINBERG

RANDOM HOUSE
New York

To Heather and Michael
and Lara and Jane

Library of Congress Cataloging in Publication Data:
Weinberg, Larry.
  Father Murphy's promise.

  Summary: A gold miner poses as a priest to save an orphan school
from closing and uses his ingenuity to rescue three luckless orphans
from the workhouse.
  [1. Orphans—Fiction. 2. West (U.S.)—Fiction]
I. Title.
PZ7.W4362Fat [Fic] 82-5280 AACR2
ISBN: 0-394-85318-0

Manufactured in the United States of America 1 2 3 4 5 6 7 8 9 0

Father Murphy's
·⊰ PROMISE ⊱·

Back in the 1870s thousands of men, women, and children moved west to the Dakota Territory. Many went to farm, others to raise cattle—and still others to pan the rivers for rich, yellow nuggets of gold. Among the prospectors was John Murphy and his partner, Moses Gage. They befriended a homeless boy, Will Adams, and then the three joined a mining camp along the riverbank not far from the city of Jackson.

The prospectors were a hard-working lot, and after many weeks of disappointment they found the gold they were all looking for. Everyone was overjoyed—but not for long. Jackson City was controlled by a greedy man who was determined to get all the gold for himself. One day his henchmen attacked the settlers' camp without warning, hurling sticks of dynamite into the tents and sheds. Few people survived—among them were Murphy, Gage, Will Adams, the schoolteacher Mae Woodward, and all the prospectors' children, who luckily were with Mae when it happened.

The priest who had helped Mae run the school was among the dead, and Mae was left to care for the orphans alone. Now another ruthless man turned up. He was Howard Rodman, the territorial official in charge of the education and raising of orphans. Insisting that Mae could not provide for the children by herself, he tried to have the school shut down. Once that was done, Rodman could have all the boys and girls sent to the Claymore workhouse, which he and his friend the warden ran like a prison. It seemed that only a miracle could save the children and the school.

The miracle came in the form of John Murphy. Pretending to be a priest sent by the church to help Mae, Murphy turned an abandoned saloon into a home for the orphans. Then he and Moses Gage stayed on to help keep the Gold Hill School going. This is one of the adventures of the man they called Father Murphy and of his flock.

CHAPTER
·•◦⧉ 1 ◦•·

It was late spring when the snows finally melted up in the high country. The deer returned to feed among the young buds on the trees. The eagle soared high above its nest. The grizzly roamed the woods once more. And the little log cabin where Dru Shannon and the old mountain man Eli McQuade lived was free at last of the thundering blasts of wind—free, too, of the great snowdrifts that had piled so furiously against its walls and had almost buried the house.

For days now the two had gone out in the morning to check their traps or hunt for fresh game—or just roam about and stretch their legs in the wilderness after the long, cramping winter.

The six-foot-three mountain man was always restless and loved to be up and doing things. Not even the bad cold that he had had for months could stop him. But his illness worried Dru, for when Eli coughed, it was like the mountain itself shaking.

"Ain't nothin' to fret about," he would tell the wide-eyed ten-year-old. "All I need is a little of that springtime sunshine and a mess of fresh venison stew."

One afternoon, when they were trudging back to

the cabin carrying a few traps that needed fixing, Eli heard a strange noise. He held up his hand and listened carefully. "There's a man a-sneakin' up on us," he whispered. "Dru, smell him out if you can and describe him to me. My nose is stuffed."

Dru's nostrils, opening wide, sniffed the air like a young animal. "Powerful bad smell on him, Eli," the child's naturally soft voice whispered back. "Like a dead bear."

The mountain man squinted in the sun and lifted the long-barreled rifle he'd brought west with him from Kentucky fifty years before. "I know him!" he said, then suddenly began to cough. "Here, Dru," he managed to get out. "Show him whose mountain it is—but leave him standin'."

Dru took the rifle and crouched low behind a boulder, waiting for the climbing stranger. Just as a coonskin cap, like the one Dru was wearing, appeared from below, the youngster fired. The hat took off from the man's mop of flaming red hair like a bird in flight.

"Thunderation!" bellowed the owner of the cap from behind the spruce tree where he had ducked. "Are you tetched in the head, Eli McQuade? I ain't the danged rebels what killed your wife and sons! What are you firin' at me for?"

"Ain't a-firin' at ye!" Eli thundered back. "Fired at your hat. An' it warn't me that fired. What do ye want on my mountain, Big Foot?"

"What do I want?" said the man, stepping out

4

from behind his tree. "I come like a Christian friend to tell you the war's over."

"Who won?"

"The Union did!"

"Praise be!" exclaimed the huge mountain man, standing up. "How long's it been over?"

"Oh," said Big Foot Taylor, coming even closer. "Let's see. Reckon now about a year or two. . . ."

"By the bear that bit me!" cried McQuade. He snatched the rifle from Dru's hands and pointed it at the visitor. "That's a mighty long time bringin' the news! What do ye really want?"

"Now lookee here, Eli," pleaded Big Foot, coming in close. "I never took nothin' from nobody. I ain't no thief—exceptin' now an' then. An' *never* with my friends!"

"Still ain't told me what ye want!"

"Well, this is it, y'see," mumbled Big Foot, scratching his matted hair. (Even to Dru and Eli, who hadn't washed in months, he looked dirty.) "Them prairie folk . . . them flatlanders, y'see . . . well, a lot of them come out last year onto my mountain. They're a-buildin' cabins and makin' noise with young'uns—and scaring off all my game!" Big Foot's face grew as red with anger as his hair. "My traps is most empty, and I ain't hardly got what to go tradin' in the towns with! So I thought, what with this bein' the best trappin' grounds an' all such like . . ." Big Foot stopped and scratched his head again, then fell silent.

"Want me to let ye set your traps here, is that it?" asked Eli.

"I'll give you half of what I catch or kill!"

"We don't need *you* to hunt our game!" shouted Dru, who hadn't spoken until now.

"Warn't a-talkin' to *you*, boy," Big Foot lashed out angrily.

"I ain't no boy!" Dru shot back and faced him as if ready for a fight.

"Well now, ain't you the testy one," grinned the trapper. "Brown as a berry nut under them buckskins and twice as hard. But sonny, you ain't a *man* yet. So don't you go a-picking trouble with them as can whip you solid." He turned back to the mountaineer. "Well, what do you say, Eli? Is it a deal?"

Eli stroked his beard thoughtfully. "Gimme ten silver dollars," he said, "an' ye can keep whatever ye catch."

Big Foot leaped into the air, whooping like an Indian. "Done!" he cried. "An' here's my mark on it." He drew out his hunting knife and threw it into the ground.

"Done," repeated Eli, doing likewise.

Dru looked on in amazement and cried out: "Eli! We don't want no strangers!"

"On my mountain the cubs don't yelp!" said Eli sternly. And then he fell into another fit of coughing.

"That don't sound too good, McQuade."

"That's 'cause I run out of my medicine three months ago," Eli replied with a sly look.

Big Foot held up a great big jug of corn liquor, asking, "This the medicine you're talkin' about?"

"The very same!" said Eli, brightening. "You hungry?"

"If you're thirsty," replied Big Foot with a big grin, "then I'm just as hungry."

"Well then," said Eli, looking at that jug and licking his lips, "you must have a powerful big hole in your stomach!" The huge man ducked his head and stepped into the one-room cabin.

After eating and drinking, the two mountaineers rose from their rough benches by the table and took to the hickory rockers in front of the big stone fireplace. Eli had lovingly carved the chairs thirty years before in the days when his wife was still alive. The same soft cushions she had made then—though faded now—welcomed their tired bodies. Leaning back, they stretched their homemade boots before the warm and shimmering flames and lit their brier pipes.

The youngster knew that mountain folk didn't like to talk much in the presence of children. So after cleaning away the table, Dru went off to a corner and lay down on a mat. By the time night had descended over the cabin, the men could hear the youngster's heavy-breathing sounds of sleep.

"That one ain't kin of yorn, is it?" Big Foot asked at last.

"Nope."

"What then?"

"Orphan."

"Folks?"

Eli threw a look Dru's way. "Scalped," he answered quietly.

Big Foot took a long draw on his pipe. "How old's the child?"

"Old enough to be a-goin' to school."

Dru's eyes popped wide open, and Big Foot snorted "School!" at the same moment.

"School!" the man went on. "They're ain't *nothin'* what you need to know in these here mountains that they learn you in a flatlander's school. Why, they don't teach no huntin' or trappin' or catchin' fish under the ice . . . or knowin' your directions from the sun an' stars. Heck, they don't hardly teach nothin' worth knowin' except countin' your money. An' with what folks like us makes, you can do all of that on your fingers and toes!"

Lying there, Dru was beginning to find some wonderful unseen qualities in Big Foot Taylor.

"Want Dru to go to school," insisted McQuade as he thoughtfully stroked his thick gray beard—a thing of pride to the seventy-one-year-old man. "Got my reasons. Do ye . . . do ye know of any such place? I mean, where a young'un can live too?"

Before Big Foot could answer, Eli held up his hand. Dru had stirred. The two men fell silent and waited until all was quiet.

"Know where Jackson City is?" Big Foot said at last. "Place where I trade my beaver skins?"

"Reckon I do."

"Heard tell they got the dangedest school down near there. For orphans. Run in a *saloon*."

"Big Foot!" said Eli, turning a hard eye on him. "I invited ye into my home an' I don't want no lyin'."

"I ain't a-lyin'!" cried the somewhat younger man. "It's where the old Gold Hill mine was, about five miles outside of town. There was a saloon there, too, only everybody lit out after the mine went bad. Then this here spinster lady . . ." A grin broke out on Big Foot's face. "Heard tell she's mighty purty, though."

"None of that talk in here, neither!" roared Eli. "Watch your mouth in front of young'uns even if they *be* a-sleepin'!"

"All right! All right! Anyway, this here school is just for orphan children and such like. That's 'cause all them gold miners and their wives was kilt at once in some fire or blast or other. There was some foul play, I think. Some real dirty doin's. But that's all over now. Anyways, there was no one left alive but them children. An' this schoolmarm—I don't rightly recollect her name—they say she cares for 'em like they was her own. Trouble is, the Territory keeps trying to close it down because it's in that old saloon. They say the children would be better off in a workhouse."

"A workhouse!" Eli exploded.

"Uh huh. Ain't that the dangedest thing? Treatin' them poor orphan children like the slaves afore Mr. Lincoln set 'em free."

"Don't want to send Dru to no school what them politicians is a-goin' to close so Dru can go to a workhouse."

"Ain't a-gonna close," said Big Foot. "They got some minister or priest or such like a-stickin' up for the school. The church is behind it."

"What *kind* of church?" Eli demanded with a worried look in his eyes.

"Now, Eli, what do *you* care? You don't go to no church nohow."

"I was raised in the love of God," the old mountain man insisted.

"Well now—every church teaches *that*."

The fire was slowly dying. Eli didn't stir from where he sat in the old rocker. And lying silently in the darkness, Dru could hardly make out the breathing of the two men. All was silent now except for the crackle and sputter of a slow-burning log as it sent the last of its sparks up the chimney.

"No sense a-wastin' time, then," said the old man finally, in a voice as deep as a cavern. "My mind's made up. We leave in the mornin' at first light."

For a moment Eli thought he heard a quick, catching sound coming from behind him by the mat—like a sob. But perhaps it was only Big Foot sucking on a pipe that had gone out. Eli closed his heavy eyes and nodded off.

CHAPTER

2

Eli McQuade was up well before dawn, getting his supplies together and saddling General Andy Jackson, his big, long-legged Appaloosa horse. Dru, who hadn't slept at all, was tired, hurt, and angry—and in no mood to do any talking. As for the old man, he hadn't the slightest objection to the youngster's silence. Besides, he disliked what he called "chatterin' away like a yeller-billed magpie." The night before, he'd done enough of that with Big Foot Taylor to last him for a whole year. The red-headed trapper was still asleep in the cabin and there seemed no need to wake him just to say good-bye. Without a word, then, they set out on the long trek down out of the mountains.

The going wasn't easy. The melting snows had left the open, treeless places below thick with mud and sludge. Even surefooted General Andy Jackson tripped and stumbled from time to time. Elsewhere the thaw had swollen the streams into waterfalls. Sometimes a great boulder gave way underneath and came thundering down the mountainside, uprooting trees and everything else in its path.

But still there was beauty everywhere—in the clear

sky, in the fresh green leaves on the trees, in the sprouting wildflowers with their soft blues and yellows and sunset reds.

It made Dru dewy-eyed to think of leaving all this behind for the dreariness of a flatlanders' school. But worse, far worse, would be saying good-bye to Eli McQuade. And then there was the bitter question that Dru was pondering over and over. *Why does he want to get rid of me? Why?*

Dru studied the man's face whenever there was a chance to do so without being caught at it. But above that thick beard, those fierce old eyes—eyes that could make a mountain lion turn and run—said nothing.

How does he really feel about me? How has he ever felt about me, Dru kept wondering. There was just no way of knowing for certain. Sure, Eli had taken care of the child after the Indian massacre. But maybe he had thought he was just "a-doin' my bounden duty afore the Lord." Dru could never remember words of love having passed between them.

Swallowing hard, Dru tried to think of other things. Thankfully that wasn't difficult to do when every minute there was something else to watch out for. Time passed slowly that way—and one could almost believe that it would take forever to get down out of the mountains. Sometimes that notion cheered Dru up.

Unfortunately "forever" lasted only three days. Descending into Wind Canyon, they mounted up on General Andy Jackson and rode out onto the open prairie. At first they saw nothing but wild grassland. Some miles farther on they passed a farmhouse. Then another and another—on what had once been grazing land for the great herds of buffalo. And all at once they found themselves on a road—a real dirt road. Stretching away in the distance loomed the town of Jackson itself!

The closer they came to the center of what Eli called "civil-zation," the deeper Dru's heart sank. But the old man grew excited, so excited that he even began to talk. And once Eli McQuade started to talk, why, there was no stopping him.

"Now lookee there, Dru!" he spouted as they started down the main street of the town. "See all them stores, one right after the other? Do you know that each an' every one of them is different? Yes, sir! Folks got 'em a store for everythin'! Why, over there," he cried, pointing at the blacksmith standing by his forge, "that man'll shoe your horse better'n you can. That's 'cause he does nothing but that same blessed thing all day. And that place over there," he said, nodding in the direction of The Stars and Stripes Restaurant, "ye can eat a different mess of cooked vittles in there every day. An' not boiled rattlesnake and bear-meat stew neither, but chicken pot pies an' things! An' when ye die—" He pointed at the undertaker's place.

"Eli!" cried Dru, suddenly breaking days of silence. "You just ain't making no more sense than that yeller-billed magpie you're always talkin' about!"

"Needn't get ornery about it," said the old man moodily. "Just a-tryin' to make ye feel more at home, is all."

"Well, I *know* where my home is, Eli McQuade. And this ain't it!"

The old man's eyes turned hard. "Now you settle to it. You're a-goin' to that school Big Foot told me about." He reached into his buckskins and pulled out the little map the trapper had made for him. "Let's see. It's about five miles out the other end of this here big city." He nudged the big gray-spotted horse into a trot. In almost no time they had ridden past the single row of stores and saloons that made up just about all of Jackson.

Realizing that there was nothing more to say, Dru fell into a gloomy silence. Eli, too, sank glumly into his own thoughts. And even General Andy Jackson drooped his head lower, slowed down, and ambled along without any spirit.

The road they traveled on now was little more than a bumpy, dusty trail made by the tracks of horses and wagons that had passed before. The sharp eyes of the old man could tell that most of these had been made many years earlier. Probably, thought McQuade, in the days when the mine was still being worked. Now there wasn't much reason for anybody to travel that way, for the countryside was rocky and too dry for much farming.

Up ahead they saw a line of low hills. The trail now headed toward the first of these. But there was still no sign of the abandoned mine or the makeshift buildings that could usually be found clustered around one.

Moving off to the right, they followed the trail up through a clump of trees to the top of the hill and then stopped to look. There it all was, down toward the bottom of a long grassy slope. The trail they were on wound off to the side a few hundred feet and then gently led down to the mouth of the mine. Then it moved on past an equipment shed, a cow barn, and a line of chicken coops to the bottom. Gone, thought Eli, were the tents in which the miners had once lived. But other things had remained: outhouses, sheds, a corral, an old cookhouse. And of course, right smack dab in the middle of everything, the saloon building built to take the miners' money "afore they could get to know the feel of it." Eli leaned forward in the saddle and focused his eyes on the second-floor railing above the porch entrance of the place. His old hawk's eyes picked out the spot where the big sign had once hung. A frown crossed his face.

It was one thing, he told himself, for Big Foot Taylor to say there wasn't anything improper going on there now. But it was another thing to have a look at it with his very own eyes. That building had *never* been intended by the good Lord for decent children to be raised in. Or to hold a Christian family. Or a good Sunday meeting. That house was built for only one thing on this green earth. . . .

"It's a saloon!" Dru suddenly exclaimed, seeing the old man's dismay. "That place ain't fittin' for a young'un like me. Why, I bet they got ladies with bloomers on in there!"

"See here!" bellowed Eli, turning red in the face. "Where'd ye get that kind of talk a-livin' with me these three years up on that mountain?"

But the old man was glad when Dru didn't reply. He guessed the answer. Eli McQuade, the man who was so silent while awake, had been known to do a lot of talking in his sleep. With a grunt, he nudged General Andy Jackson, and they slowly descended the hill.

CHAPTER

3

The building may not have looked like a one-room schoolhouse on the outside, but that's certainly what it was on the *inside*. For there, at that very moment, sat six different grades all together. To the credit—and perhaps the surprise—of their teacher, the only sound in the room was that of twenty-six pens scratching away. Miss Mae Woodward was giving a test.

Will Adams had already finished his long-division problems and handed them in. Now he sat doodling away at his desk by the window and wishing that he could *really* draw. Then he'd make a picture of Lizette Winkler and surprise her with it. Maybe he'd even put a heart around it if she promised not to show it to anyone, not even her brother, Ephraim. Ephraim was Will's best friend all right, but still some things were, well, personal.

Gazing idly out the window, Will thought he saw Mr. Murphy riding slowly down the hill. But the sun was in the boy's eyes and it was hard to make out the figure on horseback. Besides, Will reminded himself now that Murphy and his partner, Moses

Gage, had unblocked the mine opening and gone down into it earlier that morning. Will brushed a fallen lock of brown hair out of his eyes and looked again.

"Miss Woodward," he said quickly. "We got visitors."

The peacefulness of the room was suddenly broken as several children jumped up from their desks and ran over to look. The boys and girls weren't used to many strangers and any new arrival excited them. But the sight of a long rifle glinting in the sun, and two wild-looking beings in animal skins, caused an even greater stir than usual. In a trice the whole class had scurried to the window. "Get back into your seats," Mae ordered the gaping youngsters.

"Look at that rifle!" cried Ephraim. "I've never seen one like that."

"That's enough," said Mae, heading for the door. "Now I want you all to finish your papers before *any* of you come out."

"Finished!" cried many voices at once, and there was a rush to her desk.

Mae hadn't wanted to alarm the children, but there was indeed something unsettling about that armed, wild-looking man who was slowly bearing down upon the school. Even the boy with him, whose tanned face seemed curled into a scowl, looked menacing, small as he was. She glanced at the mine opening and wished that Murphy and Gage would leave off their endless search for the gold that was no longer there and come back up to the surface.

But that was not to be. Within a few moments General Andy Jackson pulled up in front of the porch and began to dream of a long drink of water.

Remaining on his horse, Eli threw one more suspicious look at the place where the old sign had been, then turned his stern gaze upon the young woman who stood smiling pleasantly at him from the porch of the old Gold Hill Saloon.

"You the schoolmarm?" he asked gruffly.

"Yes, I am. My name is—"

"You don't do the hula-hula dance or deal cards or nothing like that in your spare time, do ye?" he asked, still watching her carefully.

Mae heard a loud giggling behind her where half the children had clustered at the window. The other half, mostly the boys, had rushed out directly behind her. "No, no indeed," she replied, being mindful of her dignity—and beginning to feel as if she were being questioned like some little girl.

"And ye keep yourself dressed proper like ye are right now in the nighttime too?"

"Well, I certainly do, Mister . . . ?"

"Well, there ye are, Dru!" cried the old man as he broke into a smile. "Ye got yourself all riled up for nothin'. This place is the gen-u-ine article!"

"Well, I'm delighted you think so," said Mae, trying hard to keep her temper.

"How-de-do, ma'am," Eli said, suddenly turning so

polite that he tipped his hat. "My name's McQuade. This here's Dru Shannon. Orphan child. But smart. Strong. Dead shot. Can track a deer like an Injun. Smell a bear a mile off—upwind. Done everything I could for the young'un these three years. But now I brought Dru here to get some edges."

"Edges?" asked Mae, who hadn't the slightest idea what he was talking about.

"Whatever it is you give a body in school."

Several of the children standing nearby began to snicker. And one of them, a big fat boy named Alvin, simply doubled over with laughter.

"Hey, Alvin, cut it out," murmured Ephraim, who never liked to see anyone being made fun of. He'd taken enough ribbing himself for being short. But Alvin and a few others kept on. If it hadn't been for the silencing look Mae finally gave them, there might have been trouble then and there. Dru looked ready to leap off the horse and take them all on.

"Well, I'm glad that you did come," she said to Dru, smiling a big welcome.

"I can't read or write!" Dru blurted suddenly in the hope of showing Mae that she was making a big mistake.

"No problem at all," said Mae cheerfully. "That's just what I'm here to teach."

Eli looked worried again. "I ain't got much money, though," he muttered, taking a little pouch from a cord around his neck. "Only ten silver dollars. Iffen ye try bitin' 'em, ye'll see they're the real McCoy."

"Money isn't necessary," she replied. "Mr. Murphy . . . I mean, Father Murphy and the church take care of all that and—"

McQuade interrupted her by reaching over and handing her the purse anyway. "Take it," he insisted. "I don't believe in gettin' somethin' for nothin'." He straightened in his saddle. "Well, now I've done my bounden duty. Reckon that's all a man can do. So down ye go, young'un."

But Dru, who seemed to be holding back a river of tears, didn't move.

The old man's expression began to turn hard again. "You heard me, didn't ye?"

Dru nodded but still didn't move. The child seemed to be waiting for something.

"Well, what then?" snapped the old man impatiently.

Choking down a sob, Dru leaned forward and whispered in his ear, "Don't leave me here, Eli. You promised me a long time ago we'd always be together!"

"Whining's for pups and folks who don't try to take care of themselves," barked the old man, turning halfway around on the horse. "Now I learned you better'n that. An' that's just it—I ain't got no more to learn ye. So the best thing is for you to stay here in this school!"

"Best for who?" Dru demanded, glaring at him from eyes that were smoldering red from the hot tears they were holding back.

"Don't you sass me, child," he ordered. "An' down you go afore I have to lift ye off like a baby."

When Alvin laughed out loud, Dru threw a terrible look at the crowd of children, then leaped down from the horse as smoothly as a mountain lion bounding off a rock.

"That's better," grumbled the old man. "Now take this here carpetbag with yer belongings so I can get goin'. I'll be back in two months to see how you're doin'."

"Why don't you just say *never* if that's what you mean!" Dru shot out.

"Don't you be a-tellin' me what I mean! I mean what I mean!" Eli threw back. "Besides, I don't want to be interferin' with your edges—"

"You wouldn't be interfering at all," interrupted Mae, who was growing very angry over the way Eli was treating the boy. "Sometimes it's hard for children to get used to a new way of life very quickly. It's very helpful if they can keep up as much contact with the people who know and love them as possible. So you're perfectly welcome to come back much sooner."

"No, that's soon enough," answered McQuade as if his mind were already somewhere else. "Got me more important things to do than come down off the mountain. An' I might as well get to 'em." He wheeled his horse around and slowly started to ride off.

Dru watched him go for a minute, then cried,

"Eli! Hold on!" The youngster ran after the man and caught up with him near the barn.

"What for?" asked the mountaineer, who seemed to be wiping a speck of dust from his left eye. "Already done our fare-thee-wells."

"No we ain't!" Dru leaped on the horse, wrapped both arms around the old man's neck, kissed him, and jumped off again.

"That's what this chasin' me was about?" sniffed the old man.

"You ain't never gonna have anybody cook you a bear-meat pie like I do!" Dru exclaimed.

"You're right there."

"You *sure* you don't want to change your mind? 'Cause I'm giving you your last chance!"

"I'm sure," said the old man in a strangely tired voice. Then, patting Dru on the head, Eli McQuade straightened up, wiped his nose for some reason, and, without another word or a backward look, galloped away until he had reached the top of the hill and was lost from sight.

Miss Mae Woodward was a peace-loving lady. But for the last few minutes she'd had the strongest temptation to pick an apple from the barrel that always stood on the porch and throw it at the man. That's how furious she was!

How can he be so cold and uncaring, she asked herself. *Why, that child is a* human being—*not a stray cat!* Her heart went out to Dru, standing there in the dust kicked up by the horse, looking so abandoned and forlorn. Well, she would just have to do her level best to make the boy feel at home, that's all. She and Moses and Murphy had managed to do that for the other children, so. . . .

The jangling of the bell over the entrance to the mine broke into her thoughts. It was a signal that John and Moses wanted something, perhaps water lowered into the shaft. As far as she was concerned, the place was dangerous and should be left alone. It was ridiculous for them to be taking chances like that, looking for gold that was no longer there. The children, at any rate, were under strict instructions to stay away from the mine. She called Will aside and asked him to show Dru around while she went to see what was needed.

"I was just about to do that, Miss Woodward," Will replied and set off toward the barn.

As soon as Mae reached the mine entrance she heard a groan from inside.

"Don't come in!" called Murphy from somewhere inside the darkened pit. "Just wait there. Then give me a hand. Moses is hurt."

"Who's hurt? I ain't hurt," said Moses through his groans.

A few seconds later Mae saw the flickering glimmer of an approaching lantern. She made out the forms of two men: one white, tall, and bearded; the other of medium height, clean-shaven and black.

"What happened?" she asked as they drew nearer.

"Overhead rock broke loose," said the taller man,

who was helping his friend walk. "Moses pushed me clear but it caught him on the leg."

"Will you stop fussin' over me," Moses grunted. "It ain't broken. I'm all right. Just charlie-horsed is all. You can let go. I'm all right."

"If you are, it won't be any of *your* doing!" exclaimed Mae, who had found a good place to work off her anger at McQuade. "If you two grown men would stop acting like boys on a treasure hunt, I'd feel a lot better. Set him down here in the light and let's have a look at that leg."

"Why, Mae," Moses asked softly as Murphy lowered him to the ground just inside the entrance, "what do you know about it?"

"Haven't you heard?" said Mae. "I had to fix the leg of a *mule* once." And she gave Murphy and Moses such a look that it sent them into gales of laughter.

CHAPTER

4

After leaving Mae, Will went directly over to Dru. The child was just standing there, still staring off at the place on the hill where Eli had last been seen.

"Hi," the brown-haired boy said. "I'm Will Adams." Receiving no response from Dru, he went on. "Listen, it's really swell here. You'll get to like it. Most of the kids are pretty great. Want to meet 'em?"

Dru still didn't answer. Will was a little put off by this, but Mae had wanted him to be gentle with the newcomer. "We do a lot of things here, you know, besides go to school. We play baseball and—"

Dru suddenly turned on him. "Do you always chatter away like a yeller-billed magpie? Is that what they learn you in this school, Will Adams?"

Will lost his temper. "They *teach* us a lot of things!"

"Is that so?" challenged Dru. "Can you look at that tree up yonder and tell me how old it is?"

"No," admitted Will, shaken for a moment. "But can you divide thirty-two into seven hundred and fifty? Or do fractions? Why, I bet you don't even know what a fraction is. At least I know what a tree is!"

Dru's eyes grew cloudy, then began to glisten with fought-back tears. Will was immediately sorry he'd spoken like that. After all, he had already heard Dru telling Mae that he couldn't even read or write.

"Hey, look," he said, "I guess I broke in on your feelings, and I'm sorry. What do you say we start again?"

"All right," said Dru.

"Want to meet the kids?"

"I guess . . ."

By this time the children had struck up a game of blindman's buff. Everyone was hopping around big Alvin, whose eyes were covered with a bandanna. They jumped away, shrieking, whenever he lunged at them.

"Where is that little runt Winkler," he bellowed as he pounced upon Ephraim.

"No fair!" shouted the captured boy. "You were peeking!"

Alvin tore off his bandanna and closed in on the smaller boy. "Who peeked?" he boomed in Ephraim's face. "I'll smash your skinny little head in if you don't take that back." He curled a fist under Ephraim's nose.

"I saw you looking," said Dru, who had come up behind them.

"You're a liar!" cried Alvin, whirling around and coming at Dru with a menacing look in his eye.

Fast as lightning, Dru grabbed the boy by the arm, stepped to the side, yanked hard, and sent him flying. All the children gasped as Alvin, turning head over heels, landed in the dirt with a heavy thud.

It took a full minute for the big boy to get his breath back. He looked up at Dru with a glint of fear in his eyes, but with anger too. "You did that when I wasn't ready!" he screamed as he jumped to his feet, lowered his head, and charged like a maddened bull. Springing like a panther, Dru leaped right over him, then turned, kicked, and sent him sprawling face first in the dust.

"Wow! What a fighter!" Ephraim cried joyfully. "Give up, Alvin, or the champ will knock you silly!"

"No!" shrieked the humiliated bully, and he lunged again.

This time the smaller child didn't try to get away. Alvin caught Dru around the waist, and the force of his rush toppled the two of them to the ground. Over and over they rolled, each seeking to get a better grip on the other.

Suddenly John Murphy came charging down the slope yelling, "Hold it! Hold it!"

The children jumped aside as he rushed through, seized the two fighters, and tore them apart. Dru ducked to get free of his grip, and the coonskin cap, already half twisted around, fell off.

"Huh?" exclaimed Will. He could hardly believe what he was seeing. A long shower of silken brown hair had rained down upon Dru's shoulders. Everyone else just stared in amazed silence. And finally it was Ephraim who put it into words. "That boy—he's a *girl*!"

"Girl or boy," chuckled Moses, who was hobbling

down to the porch on his own steam, "this school has got itself a champeen no-holds-barred wrestler. An' that's a fact!"

"I really don't want to hear people praising fighting around the school," said Mae sharply. She turned to Dru. "And I'm not very happy that within ten minutes of arriving here you're already in one."

"But Alvin started it!" cried a dozen voices at once.

"Well, all right," said Mae. "But pick up your bag, young lady, and come with me."

Dru could see that Mae meant business and followed her into the schoolhouse without further ado.

Murphy remained out front and took Will aside. "Why didn't you stop the fight, Will?" he asked. "You know I count on you—"

"I would have, Mr. Murphy, honest. Only it happened too fast."

"Come on, boy," said Murphy as gently as he could. "I saw you standing around watching it."

Will dropped his eyes to the ground and kicked a stone. "Yeah," he sighed at last. "I guess I wanted to see Alvin get licked."

Murphy couldn't hold that serious look any longer. "Have to admit," he said, "that that boy sure has been earning it for a long time."

The two of them grinned at each other, and Murphy playfully mussed the boy's hair.

"What happened to Mr. Gage?" Will asked, watching Moses lope up to a seat on the porch and start rubbing his leg.

"Oh, he's all right, but we had a scare there for a minute or two. I hope the work Moses and I have done to unblock the mine shaft pays off. If we can find any gold down there at all, then it might help keep the school going."

"I just wish you'd let me go with you, Mr. Murphy. I can crawl into places the two of you can't even get to."

"Forget it, son," said Murphy. "You just stick to your studies, all right?"

Will looked down at his feet again and began to toy with another rock.

"What is it?" Murphy asked. "What's bothering you?"

"You used to let me do a lot of things for you . . . like cook and everything. I mean when it was just you, me, and Moses in that mining camp."

"You still help me, Will. Like you've been painting my wagon and helping me fix it up, right?"

"Yeah, well . . ."

"Well, what?"

Will rolled the rock under his foot. "Now that there's this school and all, you're with all the other kids too . . . and you . . . and you—" He broke off and began to ask himself why he was saying these "dumb things." Maybe it had something to do with Dru Shannon . . . with seeing her lose a man who wasn't her father either, but the one person she really loved.

"And you care for the other kids too," Will finally managed to say.

"Listen, son," said Murphy, putting an arm on his shoulder. But then he fell silent.

"Well, I'm listening," the boy told him.

"Yes, I know." Murphy laughed lightly. "I guess I'm embarrassed myself. Anyway, I'm trying to put it into words, but I don't know how." He gazed at the boy as if appealing for help. "Do you know what I'm trying to say?"

"No."

Murphy took a deep breath. "Okay, well, it's simple enough. I'm just saying that you're . . . special. And you'll always be special." He began to smile. "You can put the word 'love' in there if you want to. And if I could get Moses to write one of his grand speeches for me, I guess I could say it better."

"You don't have to," said Will, beginning to grin as he nudged the stone across to his other foot.

Murphy's eye fell on an empty tin can that had somehow rolled under the porch. "How's your aim these days?" he asked, picking up the can. "Want to bet I can beat you throwing stones at a target any-time?"

"The heck you can!"

"You're on!" shouted Murphy, dashing for the corral post. "Let's go!"

As soon as Mae had shown Dru around the schoolhouse, she took her up the inside staircase and led her to her room. It was a small but pleasant place, with a chest of drawers, a little closet, and a window that looked out on the hill. Mae always

31

brought the new arrivals here because it had a bed for one person instead of bunks. The other children doubled up—the boys' rooms were down one end of the hall and the girls' down the other. She thought it was best to let a new child have privacy for a while.

Dru looked around but didn't seem to show any interest. Mae could see that the child was still thinking about Eli. "Why don't you try the bed," Mae suggested, "and see if you like it."

"Don't matter," shrugged Dru, who wasn't used to mattresses. "Gonna sleep on the floor anyway."

Mae sighed and told Dru she was going down to the kitchen to heat up some bath water for her. But Dru insisted she didn't need a bath. "Why, just last week," she said, "I waded in a creek clear up to the chin."

That answer did not sit well at all with Mae. She had had a good strong whiff of the girl indoors. "Unless there were suds in it," she declared, "I don't care if you swam the mighty Mississippi. You're getting a bath!"

An hour later, when Dru stepped out of the big wooden tub, she was about five shades pinker. "Just look at me," she cried as she reached for the towel that hung on the screen Mae had placed in front of it. "My skin's shrunk up like a prune in the sun!"

"Don't worry, Drusilla," said Mae as she appeared with a blue-and-white cotton dress over her arm. "And you're going to look absolutely lovely in this."

Dru made a terrible face. "I don't want to look lovely—and you ain't gonna dress me like a girl."

"Not *ain't*," Mae corrected. "Aren't. Your other clothes have to be washed, Drusilla."

"Then give me boys' clothes," she snapped.

Mae was thoughtful for a moment. "Well, I guess you have your reasons," she said at last. "Would you care to tell me what they are?"

But Dru remained silent. In truth, she hardly knew the reasons herself. But Eli had always treated her like a boy, even thought of her that way. Maybe he'd wanted her to replace his two dead sons when he gave her those clothes left over from their boyhood. Now the feeling troubled her that when Eli came back—*if* he came back—he would hardly recognize her as a girl. Then he might care for her even less than he did now. . . .

Mae sensed some of what Dru was feeling. But she also thought that once Dru accepted what she really was, she'd become glad of it. "Never can tell," said Mae, holding the dress in front of her to check it for length. "You might even like being one of us females. I certainly do. Why not at least give it a chance? Suppose I hem this and you just try it, all right?"

Dru looked at the dress as if it were a rattlesnake that might strike at any moment. But Mae continued to dangle it in front of her. "All right, ma'am," she finally said with a grin. "Gonna try it. But I ain't"—she stopped to correct herself—"I aren't goin' to like it."

"*Am not* going to like it," Mae corrected again.

"Looks to me," Dru cried out in frustration, "that

ain't goes a lot further than any of those other words!''

"You're probably right," Mae laughed. "At least it seems to around here!"

Out of the corner of her eye, she saw Dru smile too. It was only a little whisper of a smile, to be sure, but a smile all the same. A moment later it was gone. Mae could tell from the faraway look in the girl's eyes that Dru was imagining herself sitting on that big spotted horse, her arms wrapped around that crusty old man, heading back with him to the distant mountains.

CHAPTER

It *ain't me!* Dru told herself as she looked into the mirror for the twentieth time. She felt like a downright fool in that dress—and funny-looking on top of it! So when the dinner bell rang, she hung back.

But her stomach was growling, as Eli used to say, "like a hound dog with a bone an' no teeth to chew it with!" Usually she could forget about being hungry when she wanted to. But that button nose, which could sniff out a bear "a mile off—upwind," had caught the scent of something strange and delicious coming from the old log cookhouse across the yard.

Whatever that dish was, she could just imagine that the other kids were already at it in there, finishing it all off. That was too much. Crossing the yard, she uttered a silent prayer that no one would notice her and went inside.

Sure enough, the place was jammed tight with children devouring food. They were seated on benches around a few long wooden tables that had miners' initials carved all over them.

"Well, my goodness," said Moses, gazing up from

his meal. "Look what has become of our champeen wrestler!"

"Now that's enough," said Mae when she saw everyone gawking and Dru getting redder in the face by the second. "Suppose we just find Drusilla a seat."

"Move over!" Ephraim urgently whispered to Will.

"What for?" asked Will, whose face was half buried in spaghetti.

"Because you owe me a nickel, and I'll forget about it."

"You're crazy," declared Will. "I never owed you no nickel. *You* owe me a dime!"

"Move over anyway!"

Will shrugged and gave up his seat.

"There's room right here, Miss Woodward!" Ephraim called out quickly—and held his breath for fear that Dru would go and sit somewhere else. But she walked over to the place next to him and plunked herself right down!

Sitting beside the prettiest girl he had ever met—as well as the best fighter—Ephraim didn't know what to do. But he felt that he had to do something, so he began to whistle "Oh, Suzanna," which even his sister had told him he did fairly well. Dru, who was staring straight down at the plate as Murphy filled it up, didn't smile or say anything.

"You . . . uh . . . you like spaghetti?" Ephraim finally managed to ask.

"Never seen it afore," she answered, not taking her eyes off the dish. "Looks like a mess of worms."

"Tastes real good though," said Ephraim, glad that a conversation—any conversation—had started up. "There's an Italian man makes it for us," he began again. And, once started, he rattled away just as fast as he could. "Mr. Murphy saved his life once when some gunmen were after him. So he keeps riding out here from town and bringing it to us. At first nobody knew what to do with those long noodles, but he showed us how to eat 'em. You got to roll 'em up on your fork. Watch!" He gave her an expert demonstration. "See? Now you try it."

Dru rolled up a gigantic ball and plopped it into her mouth. Most of it went in, but a few stray noodles flopped down her chin.

"You sure look different," Ephraim told her suddenly.

Dru stopped her chewing and glared at him, wondering whether she should pop him one on the nose. "S'matter?" she hissed through her spaghetti. "You don't like the way I eat?"

"Well, sure . . . sure," the boy stammered. "I like it fine."

"But you think I look real dumb in this dress?" she demanded with a menacing stare.

"No! I . . . I mean . . . well, you look so . . . so . . ."

"Like a *girl*?"

"Well, yeah . . . I mean, I guess so," Ephraim answered. She was getting him confused.

"Don't you know your own mind?" she demanded.

" 'Course I do," said Ephraim, swallowing hard. "You're about the prettiest girl I ever seen. Prettier even than my sister!"

Dru gazed back at her plate and continued to eat. She didn't say a word, but inside she was beginning to feel a little bit better about the Gold Hill School.

As for Ephraim Winkler, the whole world had turned upside down. For the rest of that day he scarcely knew or cared about what was going on around him. All he could think about was Drusilla Shannon, the way she looked and sounded—and how the most beautiful wrestler in the whole territory had let him show her how to eat spaghetti!

These were strange feelings for Ephraim. He had never thought much about girls before, except to be aware, of course, that his sister, Lizette, and her friends were girls. And once he had gotten into trouble for dunking Janet Faber's blonde braids in the inkwell on his desk. But Alvin had put him up to it, and Mae had yelled at him for it, and Murphy had threatened to take him behind the woodshed. Ephraim had never done it again. Then, all at once, Dru Shannon had come into the school, and everything inside of him went topsy-turvy. He was feeling good and bad and happy and sad all at the same time. He didn't understand these feelings at all, but he knew that Will would, and Will knew how to make girls like him too. His own sister, Lizette, was practically in love with Will. Ephraim decided to speak with him right away.

But Will was busy all that evening. There didn't seem to be any good time to talk to him until after Mae had called lights out.

"Hey, Will," he whispered as his friend was climbing into the bunk overhead.

"What?" Will replied, beginning to settle in wearily under the covers. He was dog tired from hours of playing.

"Are you in love with my sister?" But there was no answer, so he repeated the question.

"I don't want to talk about it," finally came the reply.

"Why not?" There was another silence. "Hey, Will. I'm her brother. I got a right to know."

"So go and ask *her.*" Will pounded his pillow into a comfortable shape and rested his head. "I'm tired and I'm goin' to sleep now. Good night."

The room became perfectly still, except for the small breeze that played with the window shade.

"Just tell me then if you *like* her."

"Will you leave me alone, please," Will almost screamed.

"Just tell me," Ephraim pleaded. "And I won't say another word."

"Yes, I *like* her. No more talking." Will turned over to face the wall and began to drift off.

"Does it hurt?" Ephraim asked.

Will's eyes popped open and he shouted, "You woke me up!"

"I just want to know how it makes you feel."

"How *what* does?"

"Being in lo . . . I mean *liking* someone."

Will counted to ten, got control of himself, and asked, "What's the matter, Ephraim?"

"Nothing."

"Don't tell me *nothing*! You won't let me sleep!" Will paused for a moment to think. "Oh, I get it," he said at last. "You're talking about that new girl . . . Dru. The one you wanted me to move over for."

"She's wonderful, isn't she?" Ephraim asked in a most unhappy voice.

"Well, if you think that way, what are you miserable about?"

"Because I don't know what to do."

"You looked like you knew what to do at the table today."

"But I ran out of things to say," moaned the love-struck boy.

"Then do something else," cried Will in exasperation over his lost sleep.

"You mean," Ephraim whispered, "like kiss her—the way you kissed Lizette?"

Will sat up quickly. "She *told*?"

"Sure," said Ephraim. "I heard her telling the girls. They tell each other everything."

"Yeah? I never hear 'em."

"Well, they wouldn't in front of *you*."

"Then how come they do it in front of you?" Will asked.

"They just say, 'It's all right, it's only Ephraim,' "

came the sad answer. "I guess it's because I'm so short for my age. They treat me like I'm a baby. But Dru Shannon—she's small too. And look how tough she is!"

"Ephraim!" shouted Will, burying his head in his hands. "You are driving me *nuts*!"

"Will Adams!" called Mae from the hallway outside. "Are you keeping Ephraim up?"

"Sorry, Miss Woodward," Will called back. "And *good night*, Ephraim."

"Good night," Ephraim murmured and lay back under his covers. But his eyes were wide open and staring at the ceiling. And though he closed them eventually, he did not get much sleep that night.

CHAPTER
6

The first few weeks of class were far from easy for Dru. Although she was nearly eleven years old, she could not recite the alphabet or recognize the letters when Mae chalked them up on the blackboard. It didn't help, either, that Alvin and one or two others made fun behind her back when she first began to learn how to sound out simple words like "cat" and "dog" and "run."

But the rest of the children were more understanding, especially Ephraim, who kept offering to help her after class. Dru would have taken him up on that, but she was more tempted by the games the kids were striking up as soon as they poured out of the schoolhouse.

Many of those games she had never seen before. But she was a natural athlete, and almost as quickly as she learned a game, she became one of the best players.

Today, however, she was very angry. The boys had struck up what they called a "championship" ballgame. That only meant that they wouldn't let any girls in it—not even the good players! What irritated Dru the most was that a lot of the girls didn't even object to being left out. They just wanted to sit on the corral fence and watch the boys! Mostly, Dru told herself, they wanted to huddle together and tell Lizette how "wonderful" her Will was. Oh, he was "such a good hitter!" And "Oh, look at him catch the ball!" And "Look at that—Will hit another home run!" It made her sick. She decided she didn't even want to sit with those girls—even though she, too, thought Will was a pretty terrific ball player. She jumped off the fence and strode away, dreaming of what Dru Shannon would have done if they'd given *her* a chance at bat.

When Ephraim saw her leaving the crowd, he announced that he wasn't feeling "too good" and left the outfield.

"They should have let you play," he declared, catching up to her. "I asked them to let you . . . but nobody listened."

Dru shrugged her shoulders and kept on walking. "Who cares?"

"Say," called Ephraim, hurrying to keep up. "Can you crack your knuckles?"

"No," she grumbled.

"Wanna hear *me?*"

She stopped in her tracks and looked at him. "Ephraim, what do you want?"

"N-nothing," he stammered. "I . . . uh . . ."

Dru had nothing against Ephraim Winkler. In fact, she thought he was sort of nice. She was sorry she had spoken roughly to him. "I'm gonna climb the hill," she announced. "Want to come along?"

"Sure!" he beamed.

"Okay, but no talkin'! I ain't . . . I aren't . . . I'm *not*," she corrected herself again, "in the mood."

"I won't say anything," he promised happily.

Avoiding the wagon trail, they clambered up the steepest side of the slope toward the line of trees on the ridge. The going was easy for Dru—too easy! Nothing at all, she felt, like climbing the great stone peaks back home. There were no eagles' nests to find, no deer tracks in the woods. No, it wasn't much of a hill—but at least it was something.

And as for Ephraim, he was feeling close to heaven climbing that hill. The more he climbed, the faster his heart beat. And the more it pounded, the more in love he felt. It was a glorious feeling now—so glorious that he no longer thought of himself as "little Ephraim," Ephraim who had never won a single fistfight or even an Indian arm wrestle!

"Dru!" he cried suddenly.

"What?" she snapped, annoyed that he'd broken his promise to keep silent.

"I—" But he couldn't get the words out. Couldn't tell her that he loved her. A sudden picture of Will kissing Lizette flashed in his mind—and he threw his arms around Dru and shoved his lips against hers.

It took Dru about half a second to realize what was happening—and even less than that to send Ephraim flying backward with a crash.

"I'm . . . I'm sorry," he babbled. "I didn't mean nothing bad. I—"

But Dru didn't wait to hear any more of his apologies. Wiping her mouth with the back of her hand, she stomped off down the hill and left Ephraim Winkler more miserable than he had ever felt in his life.

"Oh no!" he moaned as he picked himself up and slowly descended the hill. "Now she'll hate me forever!"

For the rest of the afternoon Ephraim wandered about by himself, feeling as if his world had come crashing to an end. When the dinner bell rang, he hung back outside the cookhouse. He couldn't bear to go inside and have Dru look at him that same way again. So he asked Billy Horn to tell Mae that he wasn't hungry and went up to his room.

When Will came looking for him after supper, Ephraim was sitting on the window ledge just staring at nothing.

"Come on downstairs," said his friend. "Everyone's singing, and Mr. Murphy is going to tell us about the time he was a sailor and went all the way to Bombay in India! That's the time when he got thrown overboard in a storm and got captured by real pirates from Sumatra!"

"I already heard that story," mumbled Ephraim. "Besides, he made it up."

"So what? It's a good story!"

"Want to hear an even better one?" Ephraim groaned. "I kissed Dru Shannon today—and it was a real mess!"

"Why? Did her breath stink?"

"No!" he shouted, jumping off the sill as if ready

to fight. "What are you talking about? She smells like a flower!"

"All right! Okay!" protested Will, backing off. "Take it easy. What are you so mad about?"

"Why am I mad? Who's mad?" Ephraim yelled. He had a sudden desire to throw the bed through the window. Instead, he picked up a pillow and smashed it against the bunk post. There was already a little rip in it, and feathers flew everywhere.

Will couldn't help noticing what had been done to *his* pillow, of course, but he decided not to bring it up now. It wasn't often that Ephraim went into a tantrum. But when he did, the best thing was to wait it out.

"I'm mad because I did it wrong, that's why! She doesn't like to be kissed. She hates that kind of stuff. She wiped her mouth off like she was going to throw up!"

"So then do something else, that's all," Will said mildly.

Ephraim suddenly stopped his antics. "Like what?" he demanded.

"That I don't know," Will shrugged. "Maybe the best thing is to ask *her*."

Ephraim considered this. "You mean ask her what a boy could do that'd make her like him for sure?"

"Maybe," said Will, whose sympathy was beginning to fade. He was anxious to get this all over with and go downstairs where the fun was. "Anyway, what can you lose?"

Ephraim was quiet for a moment. "You remember

46

those Mexican stamps Mr. Murphy gave me for my birthday? The ones you liked so much? Well, I'll give them to you if you ask her for me."

"Oh come on, Ephraim!" Will exploded. "That's for you to do."

"I'll do it wrong if I ask her myself. I just know it."

"You can't think that way," protested Will. "You gotta trust yourself."

"I already did that—and I just told you what happened. Look, Will, what about our oath as blood brothers to always help each other?"

"Hey, kids!" boomed Murphy's deep voice from the floor below. "We're waitin' for you. Don't you want to hear me tell one of my whoppers?" The children downstairs broke into laughter.

"So, you admit you make them up, John Murphy!" the two boys heard Moses cry out.

"I certainly do not!" laughed Murphy. "But everyone else thinks I do!"

"Will," said Ephraim anxiously. "I'll even throw in my stuffed frog collection if you'll just ask her."

"Ephraim," replied his friend, "I don't want your stuffed frogs. I don't even like stuffed frogs! But if you really want me to do it for you, I will."

"Last chance!" called Murphy.

The two boys threw their arms around each other's shoulders and went out to join their friends downstairs.

CHAPTER

7

John Murphy had taken a liking to the spunky tomboy who had come down from the mountains a few weeks before. But his attempts to come up with enough money to keep the school going had kept him too busy to spend much time with her. Still, he had managed to take Dru off to town with him a number of times when he went down to buy supplies or put something on the stagecoach.

Knowing how close-mouthed mountain people often were, he never tried to pry or force a conversation. Truth to tell, Murphy was a man who didn't mind being alone sometimes in the privacy of his own thoughts. The two of them could sit side by side in the wagon and walk through town together for hours at a time, never saying a word. But they would be as quiet and contented, so Eli would have said, "as two whiskers on a sleepin' cat."

Mae had originally suggested those trips together. Murphy, she knew, had a way about him. It was something that made people feel they could trust him, even with their very lives. He was kind, too, the way strong and self-reliant people often are. He didn't make a fuss about it. He was just there when you needed him. Mae had hoped that spending some time with Murphy would make Dru feel a little less lost without Eli. And it had worked. After a while Dru came to trust Murphy without ever having had a real conversation with him. He made her feel . . . safe.

That evening, as Murphy sat by the fireplace spinning his yarn about the high seas and the pirates of Sumatra, he happened to glance Dru's way once or twice. The look on her face troubled him. There was something wrong, he could see. Very wrong.

Later, when the children were getting ready for bed, he asked her if she wanted to take a little stroll with him. Dru nodded and silently led the way out of the schoolhouse.

It was a calm, beautiful night with a full moon and an endless spread of stars overhead. Smells of the new summer were already in the air. A warm breeze carried them down from the hillside where the wildflowers were blooming. And the air was so clear that the nightsongs of small birds could be heard from the line of trees on the crest of the hill. Yet all this loveliness seemed only to deepen Dru's mood as they walked along in silence.

Much as he wanted to, Murphy knew better than to ask what was troubling her. She had never told him anything personal before. She'd simply worked things out for herself, taking comfort only from his being beside her. But this time he felt that her unhappiness was bursting inside of her.

They stopped by an old tree stump large enough

49

for both of them and sat down. Murphy planted his gaze on the Big Dipper overhead and remembered how he had lain on his back for hours one night and actually watched it turn in the sky.

"It's Eli!" Dru exclaimed suddenly. "I'm never going to see him again!"

Murphy took a while to ponder this. Then he said, "You know, I had a lawyer friend once, back East. He would have told you, 'That's a pretty strong statement with no proof.' "

"So?" she exploded, jumping up from the tree stump and confronting him. "What kind of proof do *you* have that he will?"

"Well . . ." Murphy's answer came slowly, "I like to take people at their word. Unless I find they're not good at keeping it. Did he ever break a promise to you before?"

"No, but I just know it in my heart, Mr. Murphy. This time it's different!" She gazed away.

How is it different, Murphy wanted to ask. But he could see by the way she had crossed her arms in front of her—and that tough look she had just thrown across her face—that she might break off the conversation entirely if he did. So he waited.

"It's like . . . it's like—" She broke off when her lips began to tremble. Suddenly the tears burst from her eyes. "It's like my ma and pa!" she cried through wild sobs. "My pa, he went out to give the Injuns the whiskey they wanted. An' he didn't come back! Then my ma . . . she went for the door. An' she said . . . an' she said . . . she'd be right back with Pa an' I

50

should hide under the woodpile." Dru's body shook as if a bolt of lightning were passing through it. "But the Injuns took them both away! And I never saw them again! Then my ma and pa were dead! I wish I never met that Eli McQuade!"

Murphy stood up and unfolded his arms. The weeping child fell into them, and they held each other fast.

"Dru," he said softly after a long while. "I don't know for certain whether he's coming back or not. But there's something I do know. There's just no help for it anyway."

"For what?" she sniffled.

"If you love someone, you always take a chance. But if you don't, then what have you got?"

"I don't know," she sobbed.

"Yes, you do. Then you have nothing for sure. You just crawl into yourself . . . and then you're *really* alone. I think everyone knows that, somewhere inside. Isn't that so?"

She nodded.

"So there isn't much help for it, then. Ain't much sense loving someone and then not having faith in them, is there?"

"No . . ."

He took her small, pretty face in his hands and gazed softly into her glistening eyes. "So then you just have to believe that he loves you, too, and that if he can come back, he will. Just as your ma and pa would have if they could. You see what I mean?"

She nodded.

"I know that isn't much help. . . ."

"Well . . . I guess it's some," she murmured, wiping her eyes with the back of her hand..

He reached into his pocket and then gave her his bandanna. "So what are you going to do now?" he asked, watching her blow her nose.

"Go to bed."

"And worry about it?"

"No," she said. "An' if you tell anyone that I was cryin' out here—anybody at all—I'm never goin' to town with you again!"

"I promise," said Murphy with a smile, glad to see that she was back to her old crusty self once more.

To his amazement she jumped at him suddenly, kissed him on the cheek, and ran for the house. For another few minutes Murphy stood there, listening to the crickets and wondering why life could often be so wonderful and so difficult at the same time.

CHAPTER
8

Dru was feeling much better the next morning when she went outside to await the breakfast call. Will was already up, busying himself by the stable with Mr. Murphy's wagon. She walked over, planning to let him have it for not letting her into the baseball game the day before. But when he gazed up at her with those dark eyes of his, she found herself too flustered, for some reason, to speak.

"Hi," he said and bent back over his work.

"Hi," she managed to murmur back.

"This hitchup is cracked," said Will, figuring that she was wondering what he was doing. "The horses will break it right off while Mr. Murphy is driving it if someone don't fix it. So I'm wrapping it with wet rawhide. When it dries, it shrinks up real good."

"I know how that's done," snapped Dru. She didn't want him to think that just because she was a beginner at schoolwork, she didn't know *anything*.

"Oh," he responded, thinking that she sure had a quick temper, and went silently back to his work.

Dru saw that she had annoyed him. She didn't understand why, but she didn't care either. She was just about to bring up the baseball game when she completely surprised herself. In a voice that sounded just like all the other girls when they spoke to the handsome Will Adams, she asked, "Are you coming in to eat?"

"In a minute," he answered distantly, turning back to his work. But as she started away in embarrassment, he remembered his promise to Ephraim and called, "Hey, Dru?"

"Yeah?" she answered, turning around and putting a hard look on her face.

"What would a boy have to do to make you like him?"

Her mouth dropped open. She just stood there staring at him.

But Will had no idea of the impression he was making. "If you can't think of anything now," he continued, "tell me when you do, all right?"

"All right," she managed to get out and, turning, rushed into the cookhouse.

Ephraim was already inside, his eyes glued to the window where he had been watching them. As soon as she came in, he pulled back and watched to see where she would sit. Then, getting up his nerve, he went over to her. "Dru," he began timidly, "what I did wasn't right. I mean, without asking you or anything! And I . . . I just want to say I'm real sorry . . . really sorry."

"You mean that?" She eyed him carefully.

"Cross my heart and hope to get warts."

"All right, forget it."

Gratefully Ephraim took a seat next to her and watched her eat.

"If you ain't . . . aren't hungry," she finally said to him, "what are you doin' here?"

"Oh, I'm hungry," Ephraim replied, listlessly picking up a fork. "But . . . I was just wondering if you've seen Will this morning."

"Why?" she asked quickly.

"Oh, just wondering. There was something he wanted to ask you."

"You *knew* about it?" exclaimed Dru.

"Sure. He's my best friend. We tell each other everything."

Dru looked at him, then dropped her eyes to the table. Once more she surprised herself at the way she sounded. "Did he . . . tell you what it is about me that he likes so much"—she swallowed hard—"so much that he wants to do *anything* for me?"

A sick feeling began in the pit of Ephraim's stomach and rose to his throat. In an almost choking voice he asked, "You sure that Will said *that*?"

She turned a sharp look on him. "Why? Don't you think a boy can like me? You tried to kiss me, didn't you?"

"Yes! But that was different."

"It sure was!" she told him, flaring up. "*He* didn't get fresh. And," she hissed furiously, "I think that Will Adams is just wonderful!"

"You do?" cried Ephraim, jumping up from his seat. "Well, I'll go right now and tell him for you!"

As he sprang through the door, he almost collided with Will himself, who was on his way in for breakfast. "I thought you were my friend!" he shouted, waving a fist in Will's face. "But friends don't do this!" Ephraim wheeled around and started to run.

"Wait a minute!" the bewildered Will called after him. "What are you talking about?"

"I hate you!" Ephraim shouted back as he ran. "I hate you!"

Ephraim's flying feet carried him farther and farther away from Gold Hill. "Some friend! Some friend he is!" the boy told himself as he ran. "And who cares about *her*, anyway? She's not so much. I don't know why I like her at all. I just wish I could make her like me once, only once, so I could tell her that *I* don't like *her*! That'd fix her! I wish I could—"

Suddenly he stopped. An idea had come to him. Maybe *that* was the way to make Dru Shannon like him. He turned quickly and headed off on the trail to Jackson.

CHAPTER
9

By the time Ephraim staggered into the town, he was so out of breath from running that he could hardly stand up. He leaned against the watering trough in front of the Garrett Hotel for a full two minutes, taking deep gulps of air. Then he crossed the street over by the telegraph office and headed for the general store.

He stopped in front of the shop. Its long, high window was packed with all sorts of things for sale: boots, bonnets, canned goods, dresses—and way down at the end farthest from the door, jewelry. He moved in closer, his eyes roaming among the rings and bracelets and all the other pretty things that could be given for gifts. He had to pick out just the right thing for Dru, something so beautiful that she'd forget all about Will.

And suddenly there it was—a silver brooch! It was in the shape of a prancing horse with a horn rising straight up from the center of its head. Except for that puzzling horn, it reminded him of the horse Dru had first ridden up to school on. How it glittered in the sunlight as if to say, *"Take me! Take me!''* It was so beautiful—as beautiful as Dru. She would have to love it!

There was only one problem about getting it for her. Ephraim didn't have any money.

Stealing was not something he knew much about. Ephraim had never in his life taken anything that wasn't his. Well, once—just once—he'd taken a slice of ham from his sister's sandwich when she wasn't looking. But he felt so badly about it afterward that he'd given her half of his own sandwich. He knew that what he was going to do now was wrong, but he didn't want to think about it. Taking a deep breath, he entered the store.

The storekeeper was busy. He scarcely noticed the boy come in and move slowly along the shelves as if he were just looking around. He didn't pay attention when the youngster stopped near a certain display case with costume jewelry in it. So it was only an accident when he happened to look up and see Ephraim's hand shoot out for the brooch.

"Hold on, boy!" said the storekeeper. "What are you doing?"

Dropping the brooch as if it were on fire, Ephraim ducked past him and ran headlong into the street.

"Come back here!" screamed the man, giving chase. "STOP, THIEF! STOP!"

The heavily built man was no match for the swiftly running boy. Dodging around carts, wagons, horses, people, and barking dogs, Ephraim plunged on, his mind on nothing now but getting away. He had almost made it, too, when a pair of long bony hands reached out from a doorway and nearly yanked him off his feet.

The terrified boy tugged and twisted, but he couldn't break free. The storekeeper raced up with a crowd of people and Ephraim stopped struggling. A man who looked like the Face of Death tightened his grip and stared down at Ephraim, gloating. "Well, well, look what we have here. One of Father Murphy's little flock." It was Howard Rodman.

Ephraim recognized at once the thin-lipped, gray-faced man whom the Territory had put in charge of orphan affairs. Rodman had come out to the school many times in his attempts to close it down and whisk the children away to the Claymore work-house. Claymore had once been the territorial insane asylum, but it had been handed over to Rodman on the promise that he would "fix it up" as a proper home for orphans. Many people knew what went on inside Claymore now, but no one seemed to be able to do anything about it. Rodman and his two helpers, Miss Tuttle and the warden, ran the place like a jail. They worked the children who had to live there like slaves.

The same fate would have befallen all of the Gold Hill orphans if Mr. Murphy hadn't tricked Rodman into believing that he was a priest sent by the church to watch over the school. But there was no Father Murphy around to help Ephraim now, and Rodman took full advantage of it. Followed by the angry storekeeper and the gathered crowd, Rodman took hold of the boy's right ear and dragged him down the street. They passed the stage depot and climbed the three wooden steps to the door marked "Sheriff's Office" and marched inside.

The white-haired, bushy-browed sheriff was eating an early lunch at his desk in front of the one cell in his office. "You look real worked up, Rodman," he said with the trace of a smile. "Catch yourself a bank robber? You may unhand the 'culprit' now."

"Sheriff Beamus!" said Rodman indignantly as he let go of Ephraim. "You of all people should know that stealing is not a joke—no matter who does it or what the size of the theft."

"All right," said the sheriff, carefully rewrapping his sandwich and tucking it away in a drawer. "Suppose we all simmer down so we can get to the bottom of this." He turned his gaze upon Ephraim. "What happened, son? Want to tell me about it?"

Ephraim's fear had made him tongue-tied. Besides, what could he really say? And if he started to speak, they might see his lips trembling. He might even begin to cry. He didn't want anyone to see *that*—especially Rodman!

"The boy's silence is proof enough of his guilt," sniffed his captor.

"Uh huh? Well, what is he supposed to have done?"

The storekeeper stepped forward. "He took a unicorn brooch from my display case. I saw him. It's worth about three dollars." He studied the frightened boy for a moment. "Look . . . er . . . I got the piece back, so there's no harm done. Maybe we ought to—"

"Mr. Ardley, I'm surprised at you," said Rodman. "A forgiving heart is very becoming—but are you really helping the boy if you drop the charges? I have had more experience than you in these matters. And I must say that forgiveness doesn't work when the child comes from the wrong environment. And that most certainly is the case with that excuse for a school Mae Woodward maintains in an abandoned saloon."

"Just a minute," said the storekeeper. "I do business with Miss Woodward and I think she is a fine person."

"Oh, I'm not questioning her character," said Rodman, backing off a little. "But she's much too lax. She doesn't know how to control these ragamuffins. As a result they walk all over her. And if this child is permitted to return there instead of being punished, the others will believe they can get away with stealing too. I can assure you, Mr. Ardley, it will be open season on your store. You must protect yourself first, Mr. Ardley. Charity begins at home."

The storekeeper scratched his head. "Well, I suppose . . ."

"I won't do it again!" Ephraim blurted out. "I promise."

"That is quite true," said Rodman quickly. "Because you won't get the chance. Sheriff, this boy was caught red-handed and I demand that you immediately sign the commitment papers to Claymore."

Sheriff Beamus finished rolling a cigarette, popped it into his mouth, and lit it. "Can't just go and do that," he said. "Boy's entitled to a trial under the law, same as anyone else."

"Very well," huffed Rodman, "since you insist. I was just talking to the judge not five minutes ago, and I shall be right back with him!" He rushed out of the office and returned a few moments later with Judge Treacher.

"I would have liked to finish my meal," grumbled the judge, wiping a few morsels of bread and scrambled egg off his elegant handlebar mustache.

"You got some coffee on your beard, Judge," said the sheriff.

"Oh, really?" replied his Honor, drying himself with his fancy shirtsleeve. "Now, what's all this about?"

"He stole a brooch from the general store," said Rodman, and the storekeeper nodded sadly.

The judge opened his snuffbox, took a snort, and fixed Ephraim with a hard eye. "Did you do that, boy?"

"Excuse me, Judge," interrupted the sheriff, "but he's got a right to have someone stand up for him and defend him, don't he?"

"You trying to tell me my business, Sheriff?" replied the judge sternly. He turned back to Ephraim. "Did you steal, that, boy?"

"I—I took it," Ephraim said, "but I was going to pay for it later."

"Later don't count," rasped the judge, taking another sniff of snuff. "Did you steal it? Tell the truth now, boy. Go better for you if you do."

"Y-yes, sir," Ephraim mumbled.

"There, he admits it!" said the judge. "Don't need a trial. Don't need a lawyer. I find the accused— what's your name, boy?"

"It's Ephraim Winkler," said Rodman quickly. "I know all the children at that so-called school they hold in a saloon. And now you see, Judge, what kind of ne'er-do-wells they raise there. It should be closed down for good!"

"Well, we can't do anything about that now, Howard," replied the judge. "But we can take care of this boy. I find him guilty as charged." The snuffbox closed with a snap, and he turned to go. But Rodman gave a deliberate little cough and the judge stopped, wondering for a moment what he had forgotten. The dark look in Rodman's eyes reminded him. "And I commit him to the care and custody of the Territorial Children's Workhouse at Claymore until he reaches the age of sixteen years."

"Hold on a minute, Judge," said the sheriff, rising from his seat. He knew that Rodman and the judge were working together, and he was trying to control his temper. "I think there's room for a little mercy here. I've never once had any trouble with this boy before. You can see from looking at him that he's scared stiff and won't likely do anything like this again. He and the rest of those children up there at Gold Hill have been through a powerful lot of bad luck. They've lost everything in the world but that school and each other. So I'm asking you to give him a break just this one time."

The longer the sheriff spoke, the more trouble, for some reason, the judge seemed to have looking him in the eye. Instead he developed a terrific interest in the polished buckles on his old-fashioned shoes. "Well," he said uneasily when the sheriff was done, "you make a mighty good case there, but I think I'll just leave it to the good judgment of Mr. Rodman, here, what's to be done." Turning quickly, he hurried out of the office.

"Just fill out the papers now, if you please, Sheriff," said Rodman after the judge was gone. "The boy needs to be taught a hard lesson while he's young."

There was nothing the sheriff could do but obey. Fifteen minutes later the papers were in order. Rodman led Ephraim away in handcuffs to his buggy and drove straight off for the Claymore workhouse.

Ephraim was so numb with shock that he couldn't think. Later he could not have told if the ride lasted two hours or twenty minutes. He could not have described the countryside they went through. Or even his first sight of Claymore with its dingy gray walls stretched out on the open prairie behind a high fence of sharp wooden spikes.

Ephraim's first clear memories were of standing in

an office before a man called the warden, then being searched to see if he had any knives or money.

"Our aim here, Winkler, is to make you a better person when you get out," said the warden. "Which means you're going to have to learn how to take orders and work hard . . . to say 'Yes, sir!' to everyone in charge . . . and to be grateful for what you get. Now if you behave yourself, there'll be rewards . . . like a piece of pie or even a ballgame to get into once a month. But if you don't mind your P's and Q's, you're going to be punished. And we know how to do that here." He turned to a guard. "Put him in number thirty-four with that Stanley Simpson. And issue him a blanket. One."

Ephraim followed the guard down the long, dismal corridor, wishing for the first time in his life that he had never been born.

CHAPTER
·~❈ 10 ❈~·

Sheriff Beamus meant to ride out to Gold Hill with the bad news, but other business kept him busy until noon. He was just getting ready to ride out of town when he spied Murphy and Moses coming out of the post office with some mail they had picked up. He hurried over and related everything that had happened.

"What kind of justice have we got in this territory?" Murphy exclaimed in anger.

"This is still a frontier, Murph," said the sheriff apologetically. "We don't do things careful as they do back East. And the boy did steal it. No denying that."

"But, Sheriff," said Moses, "you know that Rodman pays off Judge Treacher with money they make off of those poor kids. Everyone knows it. Those two are cozier than the fleas on a shaggy dog."

"Knowing it ain't proving it, which is nigh on impossible," said the sheriff. "An' that probably wouldn't help the boy anyway. I'm afraid there's nothing you or I or anyone can do until they let him go when he turns sixteen."

"I'm not waiting until then," vowed Murphy from

between gritted teeth. "Someway, somehow, I'm going to get him out of there!"

"Well, make sure you don't break no laws doing it," warned the sheriff. "I don't want to have to be going after *you.*"

Murphy and Moses went back to their wagon and climbed in.

"Well now," said Moses, "got a plan?"

"Wish I did," Murphy muttered.

"Guess the first thing, then, is to go back home and break the news," his friend suggested.

The two men sat silently in the wagon for a moment. They could just imagine what this was going to do to Ephraim's sister.

"I'll tell Lizette," Murphy sighed at last and closed his eyes in the hope that he could come up with some idea for putting an end to the nightmare that had just begun.

Moses shook his head sadly, took up the reins, and called "Giddyap!" to the team of horses.

As soon as they got back to Gold Hill, Murphy went looking for Lizette. He found the tall blonde-haired girl sitting on a tree stump talking to Will and took her by the hand and led her up to her room. There, gently as he could, he told her about Ephraim.

"Don't give up hope, Lizette," he said to the girl, looking deeply into her frightened eyes. "I'll move heaven and earth if I have to. And I will get him out—I promise you."

The unhappy girl put her arms around him and

burst into tears. There she remained for an hour or more until at last she fell into an exhausted sleep.

After taking off her shoes and covering her with a blanket, Murphy slipped out of the room and went downstairs. Moses had already told the others, and Murphy found them buried in gloom.

"It's all my fault," said Dru, who had grown pale as a sheet. "He stole that brooch for me. I just know he did. And I was so mean to him!"

"Let's not start trying to figure who's to blame," Murphy cut in. "It just happened. All we can do now is hope that the church can do something about it. We should write to the bishop and Father Parker right away."

The mention of writing letters reminded Moses that one had just come for Dru.

"It's from Eli!" the girl exclaimed, making out the name on the envelope. She ran upstairs with it and tore it open. In her excitement she almost thought she could already read, until the words of the letter stared up at her like a secret code.

Moses was waiting when she came slowly down the stairs again. "Would you like me to help you with that?" he asked with a soft smile. The girl nodded, and he led her to a quiet place and started reading aloud:

" 'Hello from me,' " Moses read. " 'Hope you are well. I been fine. I am writing this letter to you because I won't be coming there next month. I've been thinking that the mountains around here are getting too crowded. Saw some cabin smoke the other day, and I just ain't used to that much civilization on top of me. So Big Foot Taylor has offered me $20 for my mountain, and I am taking it. Me and Gen'l Andy Jackson are heading off alone, the way I like it. You be good and grow up straight and true. You'll be better off there for sure . . .' "

Moses lowered the letter without finishing it. Dru rushed from the room, clutching her sides as if she would burst apart. He knew that there was no use following her. Eli McQuade was never coming back, and there was nothing anyone could say that could change that fact or make things better.

CHAPTER
·:❦ 11 ❦:·

John Murphy paced up and down in front of the schoolhouse late one evening. He was in a frustrated state of mind. *If there's anything I can't stand*, he told himself, *it's having to wait around and do nothing!* Two weeks had gone by since Mae had written the letter to the church and Murphy had placed it on the afternoon stagecoach. A few days later, when no word had come back, he'd gone down to the Western Union office and sent a telegram. *Still* no word came back! Now Murphy gazed up at the evening star and made up his mind. If he didn't hear from Father Parker by tomorrow . . .

The sound of a horse and wagon interrupted his thoughts. Though there was no moon, the night was clear, and he could see all the way to the top of the hill. A single horse came into view pulling a buckboard. In the starlight Murphy could make out a man in flowing robes with a hood folded back behind his shoulders. As the wagon drew nearer he recognized the long blond hair of the handsome young priest. It was Father Parker at last!

"It's good to see you, Father," said Murphy, hurrying over to take him by the arm. "I sure hope you brought us good news."

Even before the priest said a word, Murphy saw the answer in his saddened face. "Wish I had," he mumbled and followed Murphy inside the schoolhouse.

Moses and Mae rose from their checker game and looked at him anxiously.

"Well," said Father Parker, shaking his head and letting out an unhappy sigh, "maybe it was me. Maybe the bishop should have sent out someone else. Someone with more experience . . . who knows how to deal with these officials. I went to see that Mr. Rodman and the warden. In fact, I went three times. They were polite, of course, but they had all sorts of arguments for why Ephraim should not be given a second chance. Mostly"—he looked at Mae—"because they don't approve of this school. I just couldn't budge them!"

"Well, if it's the school," said Mae, "then if we promised to send Ephraim and his sister somewhere else . . . ?"

"No, no, forget it," cried Moses. "Don't you see that the school's only an excuse?"

"He's right," said Father Parker. "I told them I would try to make other arrangements, but they refused anyway."

"Of course," said Murphy, smashing a fist into his open hand. "Rodman isn't going to let anyone go that he can make money from. He has those children making things like dresses and toys for next to nothing. Then he sells them to stores all over the territory. He has them working his own fields, and he sells the crops at prices the farmers can't match."

"Why on earth doesn't someone put a stop to that?" Mae exclaimed.

"I don't know," said Murphy. "I really don't know."

"Well, I'm sorry that I failed you all," declared Father Parker, dropping gloomily into a chair by the fire.

"You didn't let us down," said Murphy softly. "We just have to find another way."

Father Parker didn't say so, but he was fearful that there might not be any other way. Ephraim might indeed be lost to them. "Right now," he said, "we can only pray that God gives him the strength to live through it. Shall we kneel : . . ?"

Crouching on the stairs, Will had been secretly listening in on the grownups' conversation. As he went back to his room his thoughts turned to Lizette. Someone would have to tell her that Ephraim was going to be stuck in that workhouse. He thought about his friend, about all the good times they had had together and what fun Ephraim always was. He gazed at Ephraim's empty bunk and reminded himself about the talk they had had about love. Ephraim had wanted his help and advice then. He had *told* Will how mixed up and strange he felt. Had Will really listened—really been a friend?

Will laughed bitterly to himself. *Some friend I was!* he told himself. *Even when I kept my promise and spoke to Dru, I didn't pay any attention. That's why my question about what she liked came out all wrong. It's all my fault!* Will lay back on his bed. Staring at the ceiling, he began to cast about for a plan.

It's up to me to get him out!

The next morning, before breakfast, Will took Lizette by the hand and asked her to go with him to where they could talk without anyone overhearing. They walked down by the coops, but several children stood about tossing feed to the chickens. The barn, too, was out of the question. Alvin was in there milking Esther, the cow.

"Let's head up to the mine," he suggested.

"But we're not supposed to go in there," Lizette gently protested.

"We'll just step inside the entrance."

They looked around to see that no one was watching or following them, then ran all the way to the old mine and slipped inside.

"Lizette!" he said. "You don't have to worry about your brother anymore."

"You mean, Father Parker . . . !" she exclaimed.

"No!" he cut in. "The church can't do anything. But I can!"

"You? How?"

"Tomorrow is Wednesday, an' that's when ol' Rodman and Miss Turtle"—his name for Miss Tuttle—"come to town. I'll just get myself arrested for stealing while he's there, same as Ephraim did. An' you know how good I am at escapes an' things when we play Barbary pirates? Soon as I'm in Claymore with Ephraim—"

Lizette gave a frightened cry. "You're talking crazy! Claymore's like a prison. You'll never get out!"

"Sure I will."

"Please, oh, please don't go. I couldn't stand it if you were kept in there too."

"But I've got to *try*, Lizette," Will pleaded. "It's my fault that he's *in* there."

"No, it isn't," sniffled the girl. "It's *her* fault. Drusilla's!"

"Yeah?" cried Dru, bursting through the mine entrance. "Well, that's why I'm going too!"

Will glared at her. "What were you listening in on me for?"

"To hear what you were saying, of course. And I'm going with you." *Which is more than* this *crybaby would do*, she added to herself.

"The heck you're going!" Will stormed. "Claymore's split up into a boys' side and a girls' side. So you'd be no help anyways. Now, don't you say nothing to anyone 'bout this, you hear me?" He shot her a warning look and walked off.

Dru watched him go. She stood there not knowing what to do. She felt so useless. Eli didn't want her anymore. Ephraim was in Claymore because of her.

And Will thought of her as a pest who would only get in the way. It was enough to make a body feel real sorry for herself. Suddenly she felt a hand on her shoulder.

"I'm sorry I said what I did," Lizette told her. "I didn't mean it. It's not your fault that Ephraim is so silly about girls. And . . . and it's all right. It really doesn't bother me that . . . that you like Will too."

"*Me* like Will Adams! Are you kidding?" cried Dru in a half laugh, half shout. "Why, I wouldn't trade a broken jackknife and a one-legged dog fer him!" And she ran off.

The first rooster had yet to crow at the sunrise when Will dressed quickly and sneaked barefoot out of his room. He reached the stairs, slipped down without creaking a board, and ran out into the half-light of the yard. He was bending over to put on his boots when a voice whispering close to his ear made him jump sky high.

"Mornin', flatlander," said the voice. "You're kinda late a-gettin' up, ain't ye?"

Will whirled around and found himself staring at a boy. Only it wasn't a boy. It was Dru in cap and buckskins—the way he had first seen her when she had clobbered Alvin.

"See!" she said. "I'm not a girl no more. Now you don't have to worry about me, do you, William Adams?"

"Don't call me William! I don't like that name!"

he shot back. "And who do you think you're gonna fool when they pull that cap off of you?"

"Try it, Mr. Smart Fella!"

"I will!" He reached suddenly and tore the cap from her head. Then he stared hard. Her long beautiful hair was gone! She'd cut it short—like a boy's!

"Now, this is how it's gonna be," she told him, shoving her face up against his. "I'm a better fighter than you are. An' I can move in the dark like a bobcat. An' I got as much reason for goin' as you have. An' I *am* a-goin' whether you like it or not!"

There wasn't much Will could say except, "Then I'm the boss of this escape."

"You are not!"

"I thought of it!"

"So did I. We're both the boss!"

"Oh, boy!" he muttered under his breath. "Okay, let's go."

It was shortly after daybreak when Will and Dru arrived in Jackson. They were too early to find Rodman and Miss "Turtle" shopping there, for most of the stores had yet to open. The town, in fact, was just waking up for the day. And except for the morning stage, which stood hitched up in front of the Wells Fargo office waiting for its passengers to arrive, the streets were almost empty.

Dru and Will had been walking quickly. Now they slowed down and wandered along the main street, killing time and realizing how hungry they were. Will wished he'd taken along a couple of apples from the barrel on the schoolhouse porch. Dru was growing sorrier and sorrier that she had such a powerful sense of smell. The mouth-watering scent of fresh bread coming from a big baker's oven on the other side of town was making her stomach dance. Still, all this thinking about food had its good side. It took their minds off what was going to happen.

After a while the main street began to come alive. One by one the shops opened, the entrances were swept clean, and the customers started to arrive. By nine o'clock the street was filled with horses and wagons and people walking along. *Still* no sign of Rodman.

Sitting now on the steps of the Garrett Hotel, they were beginning to wonder whether he would show up at all when Dru tapped Will on the shoulder. "That them?" she asked, pointing at a gray-faced man in black clothes and a pucker-faced woman in long brown skirts. On the woman's head was a hat flat as a pancake, topped by a flower too ugly for nature to ever have made.

"Yep!" Will nodded. "Rodman and the Turtle. They're going into the general store!" He stood up and glanced nervously at Dru. "This is your last chance to pull out, you know."

"You mean it's *our* last chance."

Dru took a deep breath and got to her feet. "I say we stop chatterin' like a couple of yeller-billed magpies and do it."

Suddenly Will reached out and took her hand. Dru couldn't help breaking into a smile. "Then let's go!" he cried.

They raced together across the street, flung open the shop door, and marched inside as boldly as if they owned the place.

Though the shop bell rang overhead when they entered, the storekeeper scarcely noticed them. Children usually had little money to spend, but Rodman, who was standing at the counter, was one of the storekeeper's best customers.

"Lately," Rodman was telling him, "I don't know why I've had such a terrible craving for sweets. Tell me, has anything interesting come into the shop since I was here last Wednesday? What do you have, Mr. Ardley, that will destroy my diet—but is so absolutely delicious that I won't care?"

"Well, let me see," mused the storekeeper, casting about under the counter. "Some candies came in all the way from England yesterday, and I haven't unpacked them yet."

The children slipped deeper into the store and began to wander up and down the aisles. A big Stetson hat caught Will's eye and he plopped it on his head. It fell down to his eyes. Dru giggled, then picked up a large bandanna and tied it around his neck. Will, in turn, picked up a man's hunting jacket with big pockets and put it on her. Opening the pockets, Dru went to the hardware section and started to pile things in—hammers, nails, a rattrap . . .

"Here, Mr. Rodman," said the storekeeper, coming up from under the counter with some chocolate mints. "Help yourself."

I sure will! Dru told herself. She found a flowered

hat to match Miss Tuttle's and plunked it on her head.

"Aren't they expensive?" Miss Tuttle inquired as she watched Rodman take a few dainty nibbles at the edges of a chocolate.

"Oh," said Mr. Rodman, "I'm sure I'll receive our usual discount from Mr. Ardley." He gave the storekeeper a sly smile. "Look what a good deal he gets from us on those goods we bring him from Claymore. I believe, Mr. Ardley, that I'll take a three-pound ti—" He broke off in the middle of a word as his gaze fell upon the little mirror that was standing on the counter. Will and Dru were tipping their hats to him!

"Good-bye, Mr. Rodface," said Will with mock politeness as he and Dru strolled by the counter. "Good-bye, Miss Turtle!" And they walked straight out the door.

"Those . . . those chil . . . those children!" Rodman sputtered. "They just stole half your store!"

"*What? No!* Not again!" bellowed the storekeeper.

Something like a smile curled upward from Rodman's thin skeleton of a mouth. "I'll catch them for you!" he cried happily and bolted for the door.

When Dru and Will saw him coming, they broke into a run, and so did Rodman. It was hard to believe the gray, sickly-faced man could move as fast as the children. But then, Will and Dru *wanted* to be caught. Still, they had to make the chase look good. Making sure he was just behind them, they tripped him with a bucketful of soapy water that was sitting out in front of the blacksmith's shop. While Rod-man sloshed about, they ducked across the street to the fish stand that was just being set up on the back of a wagon. The youngsters were two minds with but a single thought. Reaching the fish, they grabbed the biggest, scaliest, slimiest ones, then spun around and let Rodman have it smack in the face.

With a cold, salted trout sliding slowly down his nose, the furious Rodman reached out and grabbed them.

CHAPTER
❧ 12 ❧

That morning Murphy was very late joining everyone in the cookhouse for breakfast. Mae was already collecting plates from the children. "Hope there's something left," Murphy called out cheerfully as he passed her on his way to a seat.

"There is," she replied, "but where are Will and Dru?"

Murphy sat down and reached for a clean plate. "Should I know where they are?"

A look of concern crossed Mae's face. "I checked their rooms before and they weren't there. So I naturally thought they went off somewhere with you."

"Maybe they went for a walk together," suggested Moses, who was finishing his coffee.

A thought struck Murphy. "Or maybe they went off to town. Something to do with Ephraim maybe." He was reminding himself that he had seen Will crouching on the stairs and listening in when Father Parker had told them there was nothing to be done.

"But why?" Mae wanted to know. She was growing upset. "I mean, to do *what*, for heaven's sake?"

"I have no idea," said Murphy. "It was only a hunch." He turned to Ephraim's sister, who was dawdling at the table and only picking at her cold eggs. "Lizette, do you know anything about this?"

"No, Mr. Murphy," she answered, crossing her fingers and keeping the secret.

"Lizette," said Mae, walking up to her quickly. "If you know something you've *got* to tell me."

Half an hour later Lizette finally confessed. Will and Dru had gone off to Jackson to get themselves arrested for stealing. They planned to break Ephraim out of Claymore!

Realizing that precious time had been lost, Murphy raced headlong for the corral, saddled one of the horses, and galloped away.

They arrived too late, and by the time Murphy learned the details from the sheriff in Jackson, Dru and Will were already on their way to Claymore. There was nothing Sheriff Beamus could have done to help them, he told Murphy. This situation was even worse than the one Ephraim had gotten into. Will and Dru had acted as if they didn't even care that they'd been caught. They'd been as defiant as if they were the James brothers brought in for a bank robbery. Well, the sheriff had had enough. He was washing his hands of the whole quarrel between Rodman and the school. And if Murphy was thinking of doing anything illegal to get those three kids out, he warned, Murphy, too, would be finding himself in real trouble with the law.

Murphy rode back to the school, trying to piece together a plan that would have some hope of working. But try as he might, nothing came to mind.

Nothing but taking a long ride to Colter City and pleading for mercy with the territorial official who was Rodman's boss. Yes, he would do that as soon as possible. But first he would have to go to Claymore and warn the children against getting into any further trouble by attempting to escape.

CHAPTER

··❧ 13 ❧··

About noontime the next day a robed and hooded priest drove up to the main gate of the Claymore workhouse. Two guards blocked his way. "Do you have a pass, Father?" one of them asked.

"Bless you, my son," said Murphy, smiling softly and making a cross in the air. "No, I am so foolish about these things that I never remember to write for one in advance. May I see Mr. Rodman or the warden anyway, please? It is about a religious matter."

"This way, Father," said the guard, opening the big iron gate and leading him down a long path toward the big gray building.

"You have such a high fence back there," said Murphy as they walked along. "Do you also need that club you're carrying to protect yourself against small children?"

The guard shrugged and looked a bit sheepish. "Just habit, I guess."

"Habit? Oh, I see. You worked in a prison before? Does that experience help you with orphans?"

The guard didn't answer. He simply led Murphy past another guard and down a long hall.

"What's that hammering I hear upstairs?" Murphy asked.

"Workshop."

"The children are working on Sunday?" Murphy asked.

"Only some," answered the guard reluctantly. "Mr. Rodman's got some rush orders to fill."

"I see," said Murphy. "May I see the workshop?"

"Not allowed," replied the guard quickly. "No visitors." He opened the door to the warden's office and led Murphy inside.

The warden, a little man with a big pot belly, was sitting at his desk. Howard Rodman stood at the window looking out. But he turned when Murphy entered and seemed almost pleased to see him.

"Ah, Father Murphy. I was more or less expecting your visit."

"I didn't come here to plead with you, Mr. Rodman," said Murphy sharply. "I came to see the three children, Ephraim Winkler, Dru Shannon, and Will Adams. You can't refuse them spiritual comfort."

"No, of course not!" replied Rodman. "And I had no intention of it. Let me show you to their . . . room. I believe it's number thirty-four, isn't it, Henry?" The warden nodded, and Rodman took the keys and stepped out of the office with Murphy.

"You know," said Rodman as he unlocked a big metal door that led into another hall, "I think you have the wrong opinion of me. I'm not a cruel person. And I have nothing personal against the Gold Hill School or the lady who runs it. I realize that you and the church have placed great faith in Miss Woodward's ability to deal with the children in her charge. But surely you must see the result. *Three* young criminals! Perhaps now you will see the folly of continuing to support the place? But we will talk of that at another time." He paused before a heavy door with the number 34 written across it, found the key, and turned the lock.

Will and Dru, who had been sitting on the floor, immediately sprang to their feet. Standing just behind Rodman, Murphy signaled them to say nothing while the man was present. Meanwhile, he looked at the tiny "room" into which they were crowded.

Dear God! Murphy said to himself. *It's like a dungeon!* His eyes traveled to the only source of light—a tiny barred window high up the side of a stone wall. The rest of the cell was damp and filthy, and the floor, too, was cold, hard stone. There were no beds and no furniture—just a few scraggly piles of straw to sleep on. Ephraim had not risen when Murphy entered. He lay on one of the straw mats, wild-eyed and feverish. Another boy whom Murphy had never seen before lay coughing horribly at the far end of the cell.

As for Dru and Will, they dared not show their joy over Murphy's arrival while Rodman was still there. But the moment he left, they flew into their friend's outstretched arms.

"You better look at Ephraim," said Will. "He's real sick."

Murphy released them and hurried over to the boy. He kneeled down and touched Ephraim's sweating forehead. It was burning hot. "Ephraim," he whispered to the boy. "Hold on, son. It's going to be all right. I promise you."

The sick boy seemed to gather his strength. "Mr. Murphy," he murmured, "I'm so sorry I got everyone into this."

"He keeps sayin' dumb things like that!" said Dru almost angrily.

"Well, I did," cried Ephraim weakly, trying to sit up.

"Oh, will you stop chatterin' like a yeller-billed magpie an' just rest!"

"I think she's right," said Murphy gently as he helped Ephraim lay back on his mat. The good man rose and turned to the child lying beside Ephraim, but the boy shrank back from him as if in fear.

"Stanley," said Will, "Father Murphy is a friend. He won't beat you."

"Who's been hurting you, lad?" asked Murphy as he examined him.

"Sometimes the guards," coughed the boy. "But it's okay. I can handle it."

"Stanley's been here a long time. He's got no family . . . either," explained Dru. She blinked once or twice because the thought of Eli McQuade had just come into her head. "So," she went on at last, "we were going to take him back with us to the school."

Murphy shook his head in disbelief. "Back to the school? Children, don't you see, escaping from here is against the law. If you run away, why, they'll just send a lot of men to bring you back. That's why your plan was all wrong from the start."

"That's what I tried to tell them!" said Stanley, struggling to sit up. "I told them the only chance—" But a hacking cough cut off his words. "I told them—"

"Don't talk now," said Murphy.

"I'm all right," the boy rasped hoarsely. "I told them that the only chance is to get clear out of the territory to where they can't find you. California! That's where I'm going when—" The coughing broke out again, and the force of it brought tears to his eyes. He made himself speak once more. "They got us working outside the gates in the fields tomorrow. That's our best chance to hightail it."

"No!" said Murphy firmly. "Now, please listen to me. I want you all to wait. There are higher-ups in the territory than Rodman. I'll talk to them. Some-one will listen to me. First thing to do, though, is to get the Claymore doctor in here." He went to the cell door and called a guard to take him to see Rod-man at once.

He found Rodman in his own office this time, sit-ting by a window with a book in his hand and eating chocolates.

"Would you care for one of these?" said Rodman, offering him a tin box filled with candies.

"No, I would not!" said Murphy, fuming. "What I'd like is to see a doctor taking care of those two very sick children in there!"

"I'm afraid you're losing your temper at me over something for which I am not responsible," said Rodman. "Winkler was in poor health when he got here. And the Claymore doctor is not due for another two weeks."

"But they need one now!" boomed Father Murphy, who was wrestling with a powerful desire to seize the man by the collar of his starched white shirt and drag him across the desk.

"I will grant you that," said Rodman. "But you must understand that the Territory simply does not give us the money to—"

"I'll bring in my *own* doctor!" Murphy growled as the fingers of his hand opened and closed like the jaws of some wild animal longing to pounce.

"Why, that would be fine," said Rodman, "as long as the church pays for—"

"I'll be back the day after tomorrow," snapped Murphy, cutting him short and turning on his heels. "You *will* try to keep the children alive until then, I hope? Good-bye!"

A guard led him back down the dismal hallways of the workhouse to the main gate. Murphy stalked out of Claymore, wishing for all the world that he had taken Rodman between his fingers like one of those pieces of chocolate—and squeezed all of the insides out of him.

Sick as Ephraim and Stanley were, Murphy did not go for the doctor right away. He had other plans for the next day. Returning quickly to Gold Hill, he told Moses and Mae what he had seen. Then, still dressed as a priest, he mounted a horse and set out for Colter City. It was there that Superintendent Balluck, the man in charge of all prisons and workhouses, had his office.

The trip was long, through rocky country, and Murphy rode the entire night to get there. The superintendent just *had* to listen to him, Murphy kept telling himself along the way. Any kind of a decent human being would give those children another chance. That thought made him feel somewhat hopeful as he wearily led his horse into Colter the next morning and came to a halt in front of the territorial office building.

"Morning," he said to the superintendent's bearded male secretary as Murphy pushed through the door. "My name is—"

"Excuse me, Father," the secretary interrupted. "But if it's about the donation to the mission, Mr. Balluck has already mailed in his check."

"No, it is not about a donation, and I'm not from a mission," said Murphy hurriedly. "I *must* talk to the superintendent. I know I don't have an appointment, but it's really a serious emergency. Forgive me for sounding impatient, but I've ridden all night to get here and—"

"I'm very sorry," declared the secretary, "but Mr. Balluck is completely tied up this morning. He just cannot see you."

"I won't keep him more than a few minutes," said Murphy, planting himself in a chair by the door.

Annoyed, the secretary decided to ignore him and returned to his work. Five long hours later, Mr. Balluck, a balding, well-dressed man, stepped out of his private office on his way to lunch. "Eliot," he told his secretary as he crossed the waiting room, "I'll be gone for an hour or so—"

"Excuse me, sir," said Murphy, rising swiftly from his chair. "But this is an emergency. A matter of life and death, really. I've come here from Jackson. It's about the Claymore workhouse . . . the conditions there . . . and three children who—"

"I'm sorry, Mr. Balluck," interrupted the secretary. "I tried to explain to him how busy you were."

"Busy, yes," said Balluck with a smile. "*Too* busy for a man of God? No. So please, Father . . . ?"

"Murphy, John Murphy."

"Why don't you come on inside my office and sit down? Eliot, will you bring us two cups of coffee?" He opened the door for Murphy and showed him to a seat. "Now sit down and relax. Take all the time you need to tell me what this is all about. If I can be of any help at all, I promise you I will."

"I can't tell you how glad I am to hear you say that," said Murphy, vastly relieved.

Balluck sat down behind his oak desk and paid close attention as Murphy told him the whole story behind Ephraim's theft and Dru and Will's arrest. Then he told the superintendent something about the lives of these children and what they were going through at the workhouse. "If you ask me," said Murphy when he was finished, "it's Claymore that should be shut down forever, not the Gold Hill School."

"You may well be right," said Mr. Balluck. "There have been a lot of complaints about Mr. Rodman and Claymore. But so far no real proof we could put our hands on."

"It seems plain enough to me and just about everyone in Jackson that Rodman is using Claymore to fill his own pockets," Murphy replied.

"If so," said the superintendent, "that will all come out when we hold our investigation. But one must go slowly and cautiously in these matters."

"How long will that take?"

"Oh, I should imagine six or seven months to get all the facts. Then there will have to be hearings. And then—"

Murphy was getting edgy. "But meanwhile, what about Ephraim, Will, and Dru?"

"Well, I'm afraid there's nothing we can do for them until then."

Murphy stood up quickly and walked over to the desk. "You can't mean that they'll be stuck in there for all that time?"

Mr. Balluck opened his hands wide in a gesture of helplessness. "That's what it comes down to, I guess. Sorry."

"But isn't there *anything* that can be done until then?" cried Murphy. "I mean, one of those children is already sick!"

Balluck shook his head sadly. "Nothing I can think of."

"Suppose I go to see the governor?" Murphy suggested suddenly.

"I wouldn't advise that, Father," said Balluck, looking at him sharply.

"But why?"

"Because *I* am the one in charge of what is done for orphans," Balluck almost snapped.

"I don't understand you. I thought you *cared* about them. I thought you *wanted* to help. Then how can you object?"

"I *do* object," Balluck insisted as he stood up behind his desk. He paused for a moment as if to regain his calm. "Excuse me. I didn't mean to get you upset. But it seems that you do not understand the way things work in the Dakota Territory. This is *my job*—and I do not wish you to go above me to a higher—"

"That's exactly what I'm going to do!" Murphy cried as he headed for the door.

"In that case, go right ahead!" the official shouted after him. "But you won't get anywhere. The governor is my closest friend and brother-in-law! He'll send you right back to me!"

A dark gloomy rain was pouring down when Murphy rode out of Colter. It fit right into his mood. No one was going to help free those children, he realized now. No one at all. . . .

That same downpour, growing heavier all the time, was drenching the fields where Ephraim, Dru, and the other children were working outside of Claymore. Soaked to the skin, Ephraim grew sicker as his fever got worse. He began to shudder so hard that the hoe he was working with fell from his hands.

A guard, sloshing through the mud in his raincoat, loomed in front of him. "Pick it up, boy," he said. "One more hour and you'll be back inside where it's dry."

"But he can't wait that long, mister!" shouted Dru, stepping between them. "He's real sick. Look, let me do his work for him and let him go back inside *now*! I'll work twice as hard."

The guard thought about it for a moment, then shook his head. "I let you do that, then *I'll* get in trouble with the warden. Forget it." He started to walk away.

"Please, mister!" Dru pleaded, tugging at his sleeve.

"Ain't no way to be nice to you kids!" the man snarled. With one swipe of his arm, he shoved Dru away and sent her sprawling in the mud.

Weak as he was, Ephraim lost all control of himself when he saw Dru being attacked. With a wild shout, he leaped on the man and knocked him down.

"Samuel! Luke!" the man screamed, covering his head for fear that the boy was going to strike him with the hoe. "This kid's gone crazy! Come here'n help me!"

A hundred yards away two guards left their places and came on the run.

Stanley saw his chance. "Will! Come on!" he gasped through chattering teeth. "Let's run for it!"

"No!" insisted Will. "We gotta wait for Mr. Murphy!"

"I can't! I can't!" cried Stanley, and he threw down his shovel and dashed away across the field.

"Runaway! Runaway!" shouted one of the guards. Pulling themselves off Ephraim, the men chased after Stanley.

Will crouched low, waited until the closest guard came running by, and stuck out his shovel. The man tripped and fell heavily. The next guard, coming up fast, swung his club at Will's head. Will ducked in time, but his leg twisted and he fell down. The man cursed him and ran on.

But the delay had worked. Stanley had made it across the big open field and into the deep woods. He was gone.

When the day's work was finally over, the children were led back to their cells, shivering and wet.

"Sure hope he made it," said Will, squatting on the floor and wrapping his arms around himself for warmth.

"Maybe . . . maybe we can all hold each other," suggested Dru, whose lips were turning blue.

"S-s-sounds g-good," said the trembling Ephraim, moving to the center of the cell.

"But don't get the wrong idea and kiss me again!" Dru warned.

"I w-w-won't."

The three children huddled together in a cross-legged circle and wrapped their arms around one another's shoulders.

"You didn't have to fight for me, y'know, Ephraim," Dru said. "I can take care of myself."

"You d-didn't have to stand up for me either, Dru," said Ephraim.

"Well, I wanted to!"

"Well, so did I!"

There was silence for a moment. "You sure were somethin' out there," Dru said in a soft voice.

"Y-you mean *Will* was—for slowing down those two guards?" Ephraim asked in a tiny voice.

"Him, too. But you looked like a mountain lion the way you jumped out on that man."

Ephraim let out a smile that lit up the darkness of the room. For a moment he even stopped trembling.

"Will you two cut it out and just say that you like each other?" Will told them. "Then I can be cold and miserable in here in peace."

Suddenly a key turned in the lock of their cell door. They jumped to their feet as two guards dragged Stanley's unconscious body into the room, dropped him on the floor, and left.

"Look what they did to him!" cried Will, rushing over. Stanley was scarcely breathing. His face was bruised, and through the rips in the back of his shirt they could see where he had been whipped.

"Do you think he's going to die?" Dru asked.

"We'll *all* die!" Ephraim said suddenly. His fever was beginning to make him say things again. "Rodman hates us. He'll never let us out of here. And it's all my fault!"

"Don't think like that," whispered Dru. She tried hard to push back her own fear.

"Dru's right," Will said. "We gotta have faith. Mr. Murphy's coming tomorrow with the doctor. He'll think of something, you'll see."

CHAPTER

··⋅⊱ 15 ⊰⋅··

Whatever that "something" was, Murphy hadn't thought of it by the time he arrived back at the school. But a surprise awaited him when he got there.

"Eli McQuade is here!" declared Moses. "Mae and I found him lying in the road . . . spitting up blood something fierce. We brought him back here and got the doc. He's in with him now."

A moment later big, bushy-haired Dr. Thompson came lumbering out of Mae's room. "I gave him something to stop the coughing and put him to sleep," he said, shaking his head sadly. "But there isn't much else I can do. He won't last more than a few days. He's been real sick a long time. Tuberculosis."

"Then *that* must be the reason he sent Dru that awful letter!" Mae exclaimed. "And I thought he was being so cruel. He just didn't want Drusilla to find out he was dying."

"Does he know about what happened to the child?" Murphy wondered out loud.

"Not yet," she answered, biting her lip. "I just

didn't have the heart . . . but I'll have to tell him in the morning."

The first words that fell from the old man's lips when he awoke the next morning were, "Where's Dru?"

"I'm afraid I have something to tell you," said Mae, and she related everything that had happened.

"Thunder'n lightnin'!" boomed the mountain man when she was done. "There just ain't no peace in this world! I never should of left her here like I done. But there wasn't nothin' else I could do except havin' her all alone watchin' me die up there on that mountain."

"What made you come back?" Murphy asked.

The old man looked away. "Oh, well . . . just a little of this and a little of that," he said in a voice that sounded as if it contained a held-back sob. "Might of could be that there were some things I should of told ye. Important things 'bout Dru. . . ." He grew quiet, and one could almost hear his sigh. "Like . . . like she really ain't so hard an' rough as she tries to be. An'—an' that young'un can't swim a lick—goes straight to the bottom like a stone. An' don't never give her no blackberries, not even one or two, 'cause she breaks out worser'n anything ye ever saw, an' her whole body gets splotchy and itchy . . . looks somethin' awful. An' . . . well, things like that is why I come back. To tell ye . . ."

"You're not fooling *me*, Mr. McQuade," said Mae,

breaking into a wide smile. "That's not at all why you came back."

"Yes, ma'am, it is," said the old man hastily. "I promise you it is."

For days now Murphy's eyes had shown the strain of worry. But all at once—as if the sun had come out from behind a dark cloud—they brightened. The mountain man's words had given him an idea at last!

"Suppose," he said, "that when I go to Claymore with the doc this morning, we *do* give her blackberries—a whole lot of them. How long would it take before she broke out?"

"Less time than it takes for a dog t'jump on a bone. Why?"

"What if the doctor tells the warden that Dru's got about the deadliest disease there is, smallpox? Why, with all those splotches on her face—"

"By the bear that bit me, I think I'm gettin' yer drift!" roared Eli. "That feller's gonna chuck them young'uns out of there so fast—"

"I think it's a wonderful idea!" Mae broke in with a delighted shout. Then she bit her lip. "But will Doc Thompson go along with it?"

They got their answer when the doctor arrived promptly at six. "I'm very sorry for the children," he told them after hearing Murphy out, "but I can't take part in this. It's against my sworn duty to lie about anybody's disease. I just can't do it. Ask me anything else."

"That's just what I'm 'bout to do," declared Eli, rising from his bed.

"But you can't get up, Mr. McQuade," protested Mae.

"Never you mind, young lady," said the old man. "These old bones can plop themselves down forever *after* Dru is safe." He turned to Dr. Thompson. "What I be wantin' is the loan of your medicine bag, thar."

"What for?"

"What for? Why, that's as plain as the nose on an elephant. If a feller carries a rifle, why, everybody figures he's a hunter. But if that same feller walks in big as ever you please, totin' a doctor's bag—"

Moses studied the wild and bearded old man and just shook his head. "Even with that satchel, old-timer, you just don't look right for the part."

"But you ain't seen me yet spruced up and purty!" replied McQuade, staring at the doctor's store-bought clothes. "An' ain't it just lucky that the doc here growed up t'be almost my size? Now, fellers, where can I have the loan of a nice, sharp, straight-back razor?"

Several hours later a big, black, four-seated surrey pulled up to the main gate of the Claymore work-house. Out of it stepped a priest who was no priest and a doctor who was no doctor. A guard led them to the cell where the four children were kept.

"How long is this going to take, Doctor?" the guard asked, closing the door behind them.

"Depends," answered "Doctor" McQuade as his eyes sought out and found the little girl crouching in a corner of the bare and crowded room.

Dru stared back hard. She was sure she had never seen that man with Murphy before, and yet he sounded just like. . . . Suddenly she gasped.

McQuade put a finger to his lips. But as soon as the guard was out of the way, he lifted her off her feet and buried her face against his neck.

"Oh, Eli, Eli!" she sobbed. "Eli!"

"No time for chatterin' away," he declared, setting her down and reaching into his doctor's bag. "Work to be done!" He pulled out a bag of blackberries and handed them to her. "Now, eat them up right quick!"

"But, Eli! They make me break out all over!"

"That's exactly the idea," said Murphy. "Gulp them down."

"Mr. Murphy, you *did* think of something!" exclaimed Will.

"Maybe," said Murphy as he handed out medicine to the two sick boys. "But we're not out of here yet." He turned to watch the berries do their work on Dru.

Five minutes later a guard led Murphy into the warden's office. "I'm just finishing my lunch," said the warden. "Can't it wait?"

"Not unless you want it to spread all over the workhouse."

"Want *what* to spread?"

"Smallpox."

The warden looked up as if in a daze. "I beg your pardon? What was that you said?"

"Smallpox," Murphy repeated. "Dru Shannon is the first to break out. But the others in that cell are also coming down with it. This thing is going to spread like wildfire."

"Oh, come now," said the warden, trying to maintain his self-control. "Isn't that doctor of yours being a bit hasty? How do you know it isn't . . . well, measles?"

"Come and see for yourself," said Murphy, stepping back into the open doorway.

The warden's lips quivered slightly. But he put on a stern face and rose from the desk. *That* I most certainly intend to do!" He glanced about the small office as if he couldn't leave just yet. "Where is my cane?" The warden always carried one for style.

"Warden!" cried Murphy impatiently. "Smallpox is the deadliest and most contagious disease there is! We've got to do something about it before the children here start dying like flies. I suggest we hurry!"

"Ah yes, here it is," cried the man, snatching up the cane as if it were his security blanket. "Yes, yes, we must hurry! By all means!" And he rushed out of the office with Murphy, the cane under his right arm.

At first the two men flew down the cellblock. But the closer they came to cell 34, the slower the warden walked. Finally he came to a dead stop just outside the door, took one look at Dru's terribly blotched face, and shrank back against the far wall.

"Is—is—is it really smallpox?" he gasped.

"Sure as my name's Doc Thompson," replied McQuade. "Everyone in this cell has it by now. Best get 'em all out of here afore the whole place gets it."

"Get them out?" cried the warden. "Where can I send them so fast? Who would take them?"

"The church cannot refuse even the sickest of the sick," said Murphy. "But of course, it has to be legal. You'll have to sign for their release before I can take them."

"You're right! You're right! Oh, God bless you!" shouted the agitated man as he rushed away. "I'll take care of it right away!"

"I'll come with you," offered Murphy.

"No! No!" the warden screamed, waving the cane like a defending sword. "Don't come near me! I'll get Rodman to sign the release papers and have them sent to the gate! Just get those children out of here!"

Ten minutes later Murphy and McQuade carried the two sick boys through the main gate. Will and Dru climbed beside them in the back of the surrey and they were off. But it wasn't until the spiked fence and the gray walls of Claymore were forever gone from their sight that the four children really felt they were free.

Stanley, who had lain almost like a stone in Murphy's arms, was the first to do something about it. Pulling himself upright in his seat, he let out a whoop of joy. That was the signal. Suddenly the grownups and children threw their arms around each other and cheered together.

By the time they arrived at Gold Hill, though, Eli could neither cheer nor speak. All of his strength had given out in one bad fit of coughing. Moses and Murphy had to carry him into bed.

Mae was sitting by the bedside when Eli awoke the next morning and asked for Dru. "I'll get her right now," Mae said. She went to Dru's room and found the girl sitting on the edge of her bed, still undressed. Her buckskins lay across one knee and the blue-and-white dress across the other. Murphy had told her the night before how ill Eli was, and now she looked as if she were facing the greatest decision of her life.

"I want him to see that I'm a girl, before . . . before"—her voice dropped and she swallowed hard—"before he dies."

"Then there's no problem," said Mae.

"How can I, when I cut off my hair!"

"Lots of girls wear their hair short." Mae smiled.

"Yes? Where?"

"Oh, in some countries. I've even seen a few out here. Why don't you let me just touch it up a bit for you?"

"Maybe I ought to just put on my reg'lar clothes. So then at least he'll know who I am!" She was very confused.

"You know something?" said Mae. "I don't think it matters what you wear or what your hair is like. I think he came back for you—Drusilla Shannon—his own little girl."

"Did—did he say that?" she asked in a low voice.

"You and I both *know* that. So why don't you just make a decision?"

Moments later the door to Eli's room opened. Dru entered slowly, as if she weren't prepared to come all the way into the room. She was wearing her dress.

The old mountaineer's jaw dropped. "Why now, Dru, is that you?"

"Yes, it's me!" Dru snapped, putting her hands on her hips and glaring at him. "That mean that you like it or you don't? 'Cause if you don't, it ain't . . . isn't . . . no bother, and I'll just go and change!"

"Now you hold on!" cried Eli as Dru turned to leave. "Sure I like you that way! Why, you're purtier'n a nightingale's song. As purty as my own sweet wife, Becky, when first I ever laid eyes on her way back in Kentucky . . ."

"How can you say that with my hair cut up this way?"

Eli rose from his pillow. "I can say anythin' I like, you young pup. An' iffen I mean it, I'm sure a-gonna say it!"

"So you mean it?"

"Thunder'n lightning! I just said it, didn't I?" He started to cough.

Dru suddenly grew frightened.

"I ain't a-gonna pass on just yet," said Eli. "Not by a long shot."

"So what *are* you gonna do?" Dru asked quickly. "Get up and go away again?"

"Now see here," coughed Eli. "You give me one good reason why I shouldn't."

"I don't have to give you no good reason," Dru snapped.

"An' I said give me one."

"Because we love each other!"

"By the bear that bit me!" cried Eli, opening his arms wide to embrace her. "Sounds like the best reason in the world!"

It was Murphy's dog, Mime, who gave the warning. Staring out the kitchen window, Murphy saw Rodman's buggy coming down the hill toward the school. "Well, it's back to being a priest again!" Murphy cried and ran to put on his robes.

"Father Murphy!" Rodman exclaimed furiously as he stepped down from the buggy. "I just saw that boy Will running like a deer on the top of the hill!"

"He was actually *playing*, Father Murphy," said Miss Tuttle indignantly.

"Well, what exactly is wrong with *that*?" the good priest asked innocently.

"What's wrong?" gasped Rodman. "That boy is perfectly well!"

"Why, yes, and so is Dru Shannon," replied Murphy, smiling like an angel. "Isn't it a miracle?"

"But . . . I understood that all the children in the cell had smallpox."

"The power of prayer is beyond medicine," said Murphy. "The Lord works in mysterious ways his wonders to perform. Besides, it was only a rash after all."

"Now you see here!" bellowed Rodman. "You

tricked us into letting them go. I demand that those children be turned over to me immediately. They belong in Claymore."

"*No one* belongs in Claymore, Mr. Rodman. Except that you might have when it was a lunatic asylum. And I am going to do everything I can to see that one day soon that place is closed down for good. And as for *these* children, there is no way you can touch them. Remember that it was you who signed the release papers."

Rodman had had enough. "Come along, Miss Tuttle," he said, turning on his heels and walking back to the buggy. "There will be another time for settling scores. Oh yes, another time." He climbed into the driver's seat and took one last look at them all. "Miss Woodward, I'd advise you to keep a tight rein on these orphans of yours."

The mention of reins gave big Alvin an idea. Stealthily he pulled out his peashooter and let fly at one of the horses. The animal reared up on its hind legs, pulled the reins right of Rodman's hands—and went wild!

"Alvin!" cried Moses, clapping him on the back. "You finally did something useful for a change!"

"Speaking of reins, Mr. Rodman!" called Murphy as passengers and buggy went careening madly out of sight. "Keep a tight rein on those horses of yours."

"Good-bye, Miss Turtle!" shouted Dru and Ephraim together, and the whole school exploded with laughter.